(R)

THE DEADLY SHORE

Nobody knew what caused the explosion that sent the M.V. *Southern Pioneer* to the bottom of the Pacific Ocean. For Matthew King, the chief officer, the disaster was an opportunity to regain a command of his own, even if was only in an open boat with nine other men and three women. And it was the gateway to his own small kingdom, where he could be undisputed ruler — for he had a revolver. It could have been that King was mad, but even a madman takes a deal of overthrowing . . .

Books by James Pattinson
in the Linford Mystery Library:

WILD JUSTICE
THE TELEPHONE MURDERS
AWAY WITH MURDER
THE ANTWERP APPOINTMENT
THE HONEYMOON CAPER
STEEL

JAMES PATTINSON

THE DEADLY SHORE

Complete and Unabridged

LINFORD
Leicester

First published in Great Britain in 1970 by
Robert Hale Limited
London

First Linford Edition
published 1999
by arrangement with
Robert Hale Limited
London

British Library CIP Data

Pattinson, James
    The deadly shore.—Large print ed.—
Linford mystery library
    1. Detective and mystery stories
    2. Large type books
    I. Title
    823.9'14 [F]

    ISBN 0–7089–5537–1

Published by
F. A. Thorpe (Publishing) Ltd.
Anstey, Leicestershire

Set by Words & Graphics Ltd.
Anstey, Leicestershire
Printed and bound in Great Britain by
T. J. International Ltd., Padstow, Cornwall

This book is printed on acid-free paper

1

Southern Pioneer

Matthew King, chief officer of the M.V. *Southern Pioneer*, was relieved by the third officer at the end of the second dog watch and descended the bridge ladder a little stiffly. He resented this slight stiffness in the joints as a symptom of advancing age, and at fifty-six he did not believe that there should have been any such symptoms; indeed, he took note of them with a certain anger.

The *Southern Pioneer*, heedless of this stiffness in Mr King's lean, angular body, this anger in his mind, moved placidly onward, sliding towards the equator over a calm sea. The Pacific Ocean lay around her, an ocean sprinkled with islands as the sky was with stars, and the night air was warm and balmy.

The *Southern Pioneer* had started her voyage in Liverpool, had passed through the Panama Canal, had called at San Francisco and Honolulu, and thence had proceeded south-westward at a modest and steady speed of thirteen and a half knots. She was a vessel of 6,900 gross tons, nearly twenty years old and registered in Belfast. Her single funnel was set fairly and squarely in the centre of the midships accommodation like a fat, communal chimney carrying away the smoke and fumes of a compact block of dwellings, and round its tubular body were painted the gold and silver rings and the house flag of the company to which she belonged. She had a maximum speed of fifteen knots which could be attained only under the most favourable conditions and she carried twelve passengers, the greatest number allowed to a ship that had no qualified doctor.

Mr King paused a moment with his hand still on the rail of the bridge ladder. He could feel the pulse of the engines coming up through the deck under his feet and he could hear the steady tonk-tonk-tonk of the exhaust from the funnel. It was a still, calm, peaceful night, and he remembered that it had been on just such a night as this when the S.S. *Guiding Hand* had run on to a submerged reef, had broken her back and become a total loss.

The *Guiding Hand* had been on her maiden voyage and he had been her master. There had been no extenuating circumstances; it had been a plain error of judgement, and for that error he had paid with his master's certificate. It was perhaps fortunate for him that things had been no worse, that he had got off so lightly. There had been no lives lost. Except his own. For since that incident he had been in a way dead; life without command and with the galling memory of that one mistake and its consequences forever in his mind, seemed to hold nothing for him, nothing but bitterness.

He pulled his hand from the ladder rail and moved away. He stepped through a doorway into the accommodation and walked stiff-legged down an alleyway on the port side, the warm air engulfing him. A man came towards him, head lowered. King coughed suddenly and the man looked up and saw him.

'Ah,' he said. 'Mr King. Going about your duties, I suppose. Or are you off duty?'

'I am never off duty at sea,' King said tersely. 'Just as you are never on duty, Mr Meade.'

Meade gave a laugh but did not appear to be entirely at ease. The light in the alleyway caught the gold in his tightly curled hair and revealed his handsome face, spoilt only by a suggestion of weakness about the mouth. Arnold Meade was taller than King and heavily built, but King knew that he could move with an athlete's litheness. Well, that was natural enough; he was a professional tennis player. How good he was King neither knew nor cared; perhaps not in the top flight, otherwise he would surely have been travelling by air and not in a ship like the *Southern Pioneer*. Perhaps he had come down in the world too.

Meade shifted from one foot to the other. King was staring at him with a curious intensity and there was no friendliness in the stare. King's face was

4

thin and pinched, and there were dark pouches under his eyes. He had been in the sun long enough to have acquired a tan, but instead his skin had merely turned a kind of sickly yellow. His eyes looked cold.

'Anything wrong?' Meade asked, as though feeling compelled to break the silence.

'You remind me of somebody.'

Meade laughed softly. 'Plenty of good-looking men knocking around the world.'

King grunted. He did not smile, did not respond to the banter in Meade's tone.

He said: 'I'm going to my quarters. I've been on watch. You wouldn't know what that means.'

'No? Well, maybe not. Does it matter?'

'Nothing matters. Nothing matters a damn. Good night to you, Mr Meade. Enjoy yourself — in your fashion.'

Meade's chin jerked up. 'What do you mean by that?'

King shrugged his narrow shoulders. 'Does everything have to have a meaning? Is there any meaning in this?' He slapped his hand on the painted steel of the alleyway, on a row of rivets like a dotted line on a white page. 'Any meaning in the sun, the moon and the stars; in the land and the sea and the animals under the sea.' He peered into Meade's face, so close to his own, and so different. 'No meaning, no meaning at all in anything when you come down to basic facts. It is a tale told by an idiot, full of sound and fury, signifying nothing. That's Shakespeare. Sound and fury, d'you mark that? And signifying nothing.'

He had pressed himself on Meade, forcing the tennis player against the side of the alleyway.

Meade said: 'Have you been drinking, Mr King?'

'You can smell my breath if you want to,' King said. 'I had a cup of coffee about an hour ago, nothing since. Don't be alarmed; I'm not drunk. Frankly, I doubt whether I have the ability to reach that blessed state of oblivion. I have a hard head, you see. Besides, I never touch liquor now.'

He stood away from Meade. 'Once more then — good night to you. A very good night and no regrets in the morning.'

He moved past Meade and went stiffly down the alleyway. Meade watched him until he had disappeared from sight, then went about his own business. And this business took him to a cabin that was not his own. He rapped with his knuckles on the door and heard a woman's voice.

'Who is it?'

'It's me — Arnold,' he said. 'May I come in?'

'Why not?'

He turned the brass knob and pushed the door open. He went into the cabin, closed the door behind him and turned the key.

'You're very cautious, darling.'

'I don't like to be disturbed,' he said. 'Not when I'm with you.'

She was sitting in a chair at the dressing-table, brushing her long, blonde hair. Now she put the brush down and turned to look at him, so that the sinews in her neck tightened.

He stood with his back to the door, staring back at her. The light from a solitary shaded lamp in the panelled bulk-head was kind to her, softening the hint of coarseness in her features. She was wearing a flowered kimono loosely tied at the waist; her feet were bare, and at a rough guess Meade would have said that there was nothing at all under the kimono but Helen Tudor.

'I want a cigarette,' she said.

He pushed himself away from the door and moved towards her. He put his hands under her armpits and pulled her up out of the chair. He kissed her mouth and then her throat. He could feel the pulse beating in her throat.

It was hot in the cabin. A fan whirred softly, moving on its mounting in a half-circle and then back again; it stirred the warm air but did not cool it. There was an open porthole with an air scoop thrust out into the night; it carried a trace of freshness into the cabin, but only a trace. There was perspiration on Helen Tudor's upper lip and Meade could feel the moisture coming through the kimono from her armpits. His own shirt was sticking to him clammily.

She pushed him away from her and sat

down again in the chair, crossing one long, shapely leg over the other.

'God, it's hot. Now let's have that cigarette.'

He took a silver cigarette-case from his hip-pocket and flipped it open. He lit two cigarettes with an engraved chromium lighter and handed one to her.

'I feel a wreck,' she said.

He let the smoke come out of his lungs, and the stream of air from the fan caught it and dispersed it about the cabin.

'You don't look it. You look fine, Helen, just fine.'

'Keep telling me that. I need something to boost my morale.'

'Is it so low?'

'Couldn't be lower. When I look in the glass I say to myself: girlie, where do we go from here? And I don't know the answer. I just don't know the goddam answer.'

Meade sat on the edge of the dressing-table swinging one leg. He stroked his chin with his finger-tips, feeling the roughness of new bristle.

'Sure you know the answer. You're going up. Up the ladder. Up and up.'

He knew it was not true. She had told him she was twenty-five, but he was pretty certain she was on the wrong side of thirty — and going downhill. She called herself a singer; that description could cover a wide range. You could walk into the Metropolitan Opera House without any fear of seeing Helen Tudor on stage; you might find her hanging on to a microphone in some sweaty night-club and moaning her way through some pop number, but that would be about the limit of her singing ability.

Meade, listening without attention to the muted throb of the engines, heard them miss a beat, as if they had coughed suddenly. Then they went on again as before. He was thinking that if Helen Tudor had been any great shakes in the entertainment world she would not now have been travelling in a slow old crate like the *Southern Pioneer*; she would have been riding the luxury liners or the airways, just as he would have been if he had been in the front rank of the world's tennis players.

'You'll be in the bright lights on

Broadway,' he said. 'You'll be hitting the high spots.'

But he was thinking that there was this in common between him and Helen — the knowledge that they were both over the crest and on the way down. Once the skids were under you, once you were on the slide, there was no stopping. There was no chance now of either of them getting into the big time, and they both knew it. He was over thirty himself, and that was too old; if you were not in the top flight by then you never would be. It would just be coaching jobs at clubs and hotels, and after a time maybe not even that.

She seemed to clutch at his last words with a desperate, self-deceiving hope. She clasped his hand and pressed it against her cheek.

'Maybe in Australia it'll be easier. Not so much competition. God, it's the competition that wears you down to the bone.'

'Competition — that's it. It's tough.' He knew all about that. In lawn tennis it could burn you out until you felt like nothing but a shell, it was so fierce. To reach the summit you needed more than talent; you needed utter dedication. He had had the talent but not the dedication. Perhaps he had been too easy-going.

'They don't give you a chance,' she said. 'It's a dog fight all the way.'

Meade leaned back, pulling at his cigarette and gazing at her through the smoke, weighing her up. Perhaps she had never even had talent. A good figure, a pretty face, a husky voice: they could carry you part of the way, but you had to have something else besides. The figure was still good, no doubt about that. In a few years it might run to fat if she failed to watch the calories, but for the present it was a dream.

'In Sydney it'll be easier,' she said, still trying to convince herself. She looked up at Meade. 'Will you be staying in Sydney?'

'Depends. I haven't made any plans.'

'We could have a good time in Sydney, you and me. I was there once. Swimming. Bondi beach. It's nice.'

'I know Sydney.'

'Of course. You've played there. I was forgetting. But we could have a good time, couldn't we?'

'Maybe.'

'But we could, couldn't we?' She was looking at him anxiously now. She wanted more than a maybe.

'You're right,' he said. 'We could have a good time. But you know how it'll be — you with your job, me playing tennis. Mightn't be so easy to fit in.'

He wondered just how seriously she was taking this thing. Was she perhaps falling in love with him? That would be the devil; there was no room for that, not in his luggage. Or maybe she was clutching at him as a lifebelt now that she felt herself sinking. If so, she would have to think again. He was no lifebelt, not for her.

He swung himself off the dressing-table and dragged at his shirt. She stood up and stubbed out her cigarette in a brass ash-tray. A thin spiral of pungent smoke rose from the wreckage.

'It's hot,' she said again. 'You'd think they'd have air-conditioning.'

'Not in an old tub like this. Costs money.'

'What doesn't?'

She let the kimono slip from her shoulders, and it was as he had guessed: there was nothing under the kimono but Helen Tudor.

It occurred to him that she would look pretty good on Bondi beach if it ever came to that.

2

First Watch

Christopher Barlow lay on his bunk reading a book and listening with half an ear to the muffled noises of a ship in the first watch of the night. He knew them all: the rattle of his wardrobe door vibrating in sympathy with the engines, a slight creaking of timbers, the clanking of the rudder chains in the steerage just aft of his cabin, a man humming softly to himself as he padded past in the alleyway outside.

The heat was intense in that little steel box of a cabin, but it did not greatly bother Chris Barlow. He had a lean, bony frame, dried out long ago by sun and wind and salt, so that at the age of thirty he had a kind of brown, preserved look about him. His hair was bleached to the colour of ripe barley and his eyes were such a pale blue that they looked as though they had been bleached also.

The cabin door was on the hook and light from a forty watt bulb revealed the bare white sides of the cabin. It revealed oil-skins hanging on the door, gumboots pushed away in one corner, a chair, a wash-basin, a mirror screwed to the bulk-head opposite his bunk, two empty beer cans, a towel marked with the name of the shipping line and a porthole wide open.

Barlow dropped the book, swung his legs over the side of the bunk and dropped lightly to the floor. He was wearing a blue cotton shirt and denim trousers. Now he pulled on a pair of canvas shoes, found a black, bitten-down pipe, filled it with tobacco from a flat tin, lit it, switched the light off and went out into the alleyway. The alleyway was deserted; it had a smell of new paint and old cooking, of oil and disinfectant; it was hot out there too.

Barlow went up on deck where the air was fresher. He walked round to the stern and stood for a while leaning on the taffrail, smoking his pipe and watching the phosphorescent glitter of the wake. He felt a strange sense of alertness, as

16

though he were waiting for something to happen; it was like a faint tingling of the nerves.

'Damn nonsense,' he said aloud. It was no part of his job to be getting premonitions; he was a bosun, not a clairvoyant. Nevertheless, the feeling persisted.

He pushed himself away from the taffrail and came round the poop deckhouse to the head of the ladder leading down to the after main deck. He could see the dark squares of the hatch covers and his nostrils caught the sharp, biting fumes drifting back from the funnel, the exhaust gases of the diesels.

He descended the ladder and walked along the main deck, and it was like walking along a steel pavement; there was scarcely any movement at all, not enough to upset even the weakest of stomachs. He came to the ladder leading up to the midships accommodation, climbed it and went in under the shadow of the boat-deck.

He could see somebody standing by the port rails. He tapped the rails as he came up and the shadowy figure turned to face him.

'So you're taking a breath of air too, Miss Summers.'

'Oh, it's you, Mr Barlow. You gave me a shock. I didn't hear you coming.'

'I move pretty silently,' Barlow said. 'Sorry to scare you though.'

He could see the faint outline of her face and he could fill in the details from memory. Katherine Summers was small and dark and none too sure of herself. Barlow knew her well because she had been on board ever since the ship had left England, and he knew quite a lot about her because she had confided in him. He knew that she was twenty-five, that she worked in an office and that she had saved up for seven years to pay for this voyage round the world.

It was in San Francisco that she had told him all about herself. He had run across her quite by chance, looking so obviously lost and lonely that he had taken pity and had offered to show her round the town. It was an impulse that he had half regretted almost immediately

18

afterwards, but it had been too late then because she had accepted the offer with a kind of breathless eagerness. He had been stuck with her for the rest of the day.

Not that there had been any great hardship in that. Katherine Summers was not the kind of girl a man would be ashamed to be seen with. She was easy to look at even if she was not the type that men whistled at in the street. And then the same thing had happened in Honolulu, and there could be no doubt at all that, though he still called her Miss Summers and tried to keep things on an impersonal basis, she was getting certain romantic ideas into her head. And the devil of it was that he was getting some ideas into his own head also, much as he might try to keep them out.

He sucked at his pipe and the tobacco glowed in the bowl. He heard her voice again.

'I hope I'm not being a bother to you, Mr Barlow.'

'In what way?'

'You don't have to waste your time with me ashore. I expect you have far more interesting things to do. When we get to Sydney I'll look after myself.'

'If you'd prefer it that way.'

'Oh, no,' she said quickly. 'I wouldn't prefer it. It's just that I don't want you to think you have to accompany me.'

'You think I've been doing it from a sense of duty?'

'I don't know what to think.'

'Then don't,' he said. 'And I'll be happy to go ashore with you in Sydney if you aren't fed up with my company.'

'Oh, no,' she said again. 'I'd never be tired of that.'

★ ★ ★

Stephen Walsh was fifty-four; he was five feet seven inches tall and he weighed about thirteen stone, which was at least two and a half stone too much. Most of this excess weight seemed to gather around his waist; it travelled in front of him when he walked, and when he lay on his back it formed a small hill of flesh that rose and fell in time with his somewhat laboured breathing.

20

Walsh was senior partner in a plastics firm which owned a small factory in one of the new towns not far from London. The factory turned out ash-trays, door-knobs, vases, saucepan handles and various other articles of a similar nature. It was a thriving little business, not large enough to have become impersonal, not too small to provide Walsh and his partner, Jackson, with a comfortable income. If it had not been for the iniquitously high level of taxation they might have been doing even better.

Walsh gasped for air; it was like a furnace inside this cabin; he could feel the sweat rolling out of him. Although it was quite early he had already changed into pyjamas and was lying on his bunk, telling himself what a fool he had been to come in this ship; he would have been far more usefully employed seeing to the business. He ought never to have listened to that specialist. Run-down indeed! In need of a long sea voyage to get away from it all. Piffle! Ten to one Jackson had put the fellow up to it; he had always wanted to have a free hand.

'Lord!' Walsh muttered. 'What a hot-box.'

He wondered what kind of a state things would be in when he got back to England. If he got back. The way he was feeling now, it seemed not at all unlikely that he would fail to survive the trip.

'You have a go round the world on a cargo-passenger liner,' Jackson had said. 'Months and months with nothing to do but rest your bones and see the sights. Wish I was coming with you.'

Walsh snorted and wiped the sweat off his forehead. Jackson would have been welcome to a change of places with him now. He was bored. There was no one you could talk business to, not a single one who seemed to have heard of Walsh and Jackson's Plastics. And there was nothing else really worth talking about.

He was interrupted in his musing by the sound of a knock on the cabin door. He wiped the sweat from his face with a handkerchief, smoothed his hair back over the bald patch on the crown of his head, and said: 'Come in.'

He had not locked the door; he had in

fact left it on the hook. He had read about disasters at sea, about cabin doors being jammed, trapping people while the ship sank, and he had no intention of allowing himself to be caught in such a situation as that.

A hand lifted the hook and the door was pushed inwards. A woman came into the cabin and closed the door behind her. Walsh saw that it was the stewardess, Miss Partridge, with whom he had occasionally exchanged a few words. He raised himself on an elbow and stared at her. She looked, he thought, rather nervous.

'Is something wrong?'

Evelyn Partridge was a tall, thin woman with a long, narrow face and ginger hair. She was wearing a white linen dress drawn in at the waist by a wide cotton belt and fastened in front by a vertical row of blue buttons.

'I'm sorry if I disturbed you,' she said. 'I didn't think you'd have gone to bed.'

'I haven't,' Walsh said. 'That is, not to sleep.'

He realized suddenly that his pyjama jacket was gaping open. He pulled it across his chest and buttoned it. The stewardess watched him in silence and he felt ill at ease.

'Nothing's happened, I hope. The ship — '

'To the ship? No. Why should anything happen to the ship?'

'I don't know.' His glance strayed momentarily to the life-jacket hanging on the door. 'I thought it might have been an emergency.'

'Oh, no, sir, nothing of that sort. I just wanted to talk to you.'

'Talk to me?' He wondered for a moment whether she was perhaps a shade unbalanced. 'What about?'

She was standing with her back to the door, her hands clasped in front of her, the fingers twisting nervously. 'I hope you aren't angry, sir.'

'No, not angry. Just surprised. And curious. Frankly, I don't see why you should want to talk to me at all.'

'It's a business matter, sir.'

'Business. Oh, I see. Well, hadn't you better sit down? I'm not in a very businesslike outfit but you'll have to excuse that. These aren't exactly office hours, are they?'

While she was moving across the cabin to a chair he pulled himself up in the bunk and took a cigar from a box.

'You don't object to my smoking?'

'No, of course not. Not at all. It wouldn't be my place to object, would it?'

'Nonsense. If you don't like the smoke, say so. Some women can't stand it.'

'I don't mind, sir. Not in the least.'

She was sitting now, hands folded on her lap, her feet together. He noticed that her face was dusted with freckles and that some of the skin had peeled from the tip of her nose. It was a sharply pointed nose, a little pinched.

'Would you like a cigarette?'

'No, thank you. I never smoke.'

He struck a match and got the cigar going. Aromatic smoke pervaded the cabin and drifted away towards the open porthole.

'Business now,' Walsh prompted. 'What kind of business?'

'I understand you own a factory — '

'A small one. Partly.' Walsh was

deprecatory. He did not wish to give the impression that he was a millionaire. He suspected that this might be leading up to a touch. He had never had to refuse a touch in his pyjamas in a ship's cabin, but he felt capable of doing so even in such conditions. When it came to a question of holding on to money Stephen Walsh was like the strong-room of a bank; nothing short of a blasting operation could get it out of him. But he was willing to talk. An abstract discussion cost nothing.

Miss Partridge swallowed audibly and said with some hesitation: 'It's about my nephew Albert.'

She halted there, as though she had come to an impassable barrier. Stephen Walsh, his cigar drawing satisfactorily, regarded her almost with benevolence. At least it was helping to pass the time; and she was not such a bad-looking woman really; in a way not unlike his late wife, though thinner; Marian had had the same sort of hair, the same cast of features.

'What about your nephew?' he said, taking the cigar from his thick, pale lips.

He had demolished the barrier. Miss

Partridge went past it with a rush.

'Albert's twenty. He's a good boy but he doesn't seem able to settle down. Of course it's been hard for him, losing his father when he was a child. My sister's done all she could, but it's not like having a father, not for a boy. He's clever though. I'm sure he'd get on well if only he could get a really good start. With some firm where his talents were appreciated, if you see what I mean.'

So it was not to be a touch, not exactly. Walsh breathed more freely. He had never had any doubts about his powers of resistance, but it was more pleasant not to have to refuse. He saw what Miss Partridge was aiming at, but since this was something that would not call for any parting with hard cash, nor even for immediate action of any kind, he was not worried. His voice was bland.

'Go on please. I am listening.'

Miss Partridge swallowed again and went on. 'There must be lots of openings in a business like yours, Mr Walsh. I'm sure you need young, energetic men.'

'Is Albert energetic?'

27

'Oh, yes, really he is. I'm sure you'd never regret giving him a chance — never.'

'Well, I'll think it over,' Walsh said. 'Nothing I can do at present, of course. But when we get back to England I'll see what I can do.'

He could see no reason to tell her that he proposed to do precisely nothing. If her precious nephew had been any good he would have found himself a job and stuck to it. Walsh believed he had a pretty shrewd idea of what Master Albert was like — shiftless, expecting the world's goods to drop into his lap. He knew the type; he had seen too many of them. But there was no need to tell the woman that. He drew smoke from the cigar and let it float away from him, thinning as it went.

'Yes,' he said, 'I think something might be arranged.'

She stood up. 'You're very kind, sir. I don't know how to thank you.'

'Don't try. It's just business after all. To my advantage as well as the boy's. That is if he turns out to be worth his salt.'

'He will, he will.'

She was still standing there when the

whole cabin seemed to give a sudden leap upwards and sideways. The light went out and Walsh felt the woman fall on top of him. He heard a loud rumbling noise and fear blazed up in his mind.

'It's happened. My God, it's happened.'

3

Crack-Up

The explosion occurred in the engine-room, and those duty engineers and greasers who were not killed outright by it were caught by a blast of fire and hot gases that overtook them before they could reach the ladders and climb to the safety of the upper deck.

A series of subsidiary explosions followed closely on the first, and the fire spread quickly to other parts of the ship. It attacked the superstructure amidships with particular ferocity, and Captain Devons soon realized that if any boats were to be got safely away they would have to be launched at once. It was no time for hesitation.

The first explosion had done a number of things besides killing the men in the engine-room. It had cut off the ship's lighting, it had started the fire, and it had blown a hole in the starboard side just below the water-line. Perhaps it was of minor importance that it should also have flung Miss Partridge across Stephen Walsh's yielding stomach.

For a few moments Walsh struggled frantically under Miss Partridge's weight in the hot and humid darkness of the cabin. He did not realize that his struggles were in fact hindering her in her efforts to get back on her feet, for he had put his arms round her neck and was pulling her down towards him. Thus for a time they lay on the bunk, neither able to get up, their faces close together and their breath mingling as they gasped for air.

Walsh felt as though he were being suffocated. He heard the secondary explosions following, one after another, and he felt the cabin vibrate with the shock. Something crashed to the floor and splintered; it might have been the glass tumbler that he had used earlier, but in the darkness he could not be certain.

Suddenly the pressure on his chest and stomach was released; Miss Partridge had at last succeeded in freeing herself from

his insane clasp and was able to stand up.
'What is it?' he asked. 'For God's sake, what's happened?'

Miss Partridge was still breathing rapidly. 'Something must have exploded.'

'What could have exploded?' Walsh's voice rose in anger. He was frightened, and his fright turned to rage. This was the last straw. It was bad enough that he should have been persuaded, indeed almost coerced, into coming on this wretched voyage at all; and now it was apparently to end in disaster.

'What could have exploded?' he repeated. 'Have they started another war? Was it a torpedo? A mine?'

He reached out a hand and found Miss Partridge's skirt. He tugged at it.

She had regained control of her voice. It sounded very calm in contrast with Walsh's anger. 'I don't know. No doubt we shall soon find out. It may be nothing to worry about.'

'Nothing to worry about!' He swung his legs off the bunk and put his feet on the floor. A splinter of glass pricked his left foot and he gave a cry of pain.

'What's the matter, Mr Walsh? Are you hurt?'

He sat back on the bunk, holding his foot. He could feel the blood on his fingers, and he was afraid of blood; it made him sick.

'I've cut my foot.'

Miss Partridge said abruptly: 'The engines have stopped.'

Walsh said: 'My foot's bleeding. Can't you do something?'

'I can't do anything about it in the dark.'

Walsh noticed now that something had happened to the cabin. The floor was sloping and the slope was increasing. Miss Partridge noticed it also; she seemed to have lost any interest that she might have had in his foot.

'The ship's taken a list.'

Walsh remembered his electric torch. He found it and switched it on. By its light he could see the glass scattered on the floor.

'We'd better get out of here,' Miss Partridge said.

She moved towards the door and Walsh

33

yelled: 'Don't leave me. Wait. Wait a minute. I'm coming.'

She paused with her hand on the door-knob, and Walsh, ignoring the cut, pushed his feet into a pair of slippers. He slipped a silk dressing-gown over his shoulders and the life-jacket over the dressing-gown.

'All right then. I'm ready.'

Miss Partridge turned the knob and pulled, but the door remained closed.

'The door's stuck. I can't open it.'

Panic flared up in Walsh again and he shouted at her accusingly: 'Why did you shut it? It's your fault. You must want to kill me.'

She answered him sharply; her voice seemed to cut through his fear. 'You're being ridiculous, Mr Walsh. Please be calm. Perhaps you can pull the door open. You're stronger.'

He doubted whether he was stronger; he felt no strength at all. It was as though his bones had melted in the heat, leaving only a soft, gelatinous substance that would tremble at the merest touch. Nevertheless, he handed the torch to Miss

Partridge and gripped the door-knob in both hands. The door resisted his efforts and the sweat on his hands prevented him from getting a firm hold.

He tried again. He was sobbing with the effort. And then he realized that he had not turned the knob. When he did so the door opened suddenly and he fell heavily backwards on to the sloping floor. For a moment he was quite dazed, but he felt Miss Partridge's hand on his arm as she tried to pull him to his feet.

'Hurry, Mr Walsh, hurry. Can't you smell it?'

'Smell what?'

'The smoke. There's a fire somewhere.'

The scent of it caught suddenly at his own nostrils and he understood the drift of what she was saying. Somewhere in the ship a fire was burning, spreading. Perhaps already they were caught. He scrambled to his feet.

In the alleyway an emergency light was on and they could see a thin wreath of smoke moving sluggishly. It was impossible to say where it was coming from; it just seemed to be forming spontaneously and it carried an odour of burning paint.

A little group of bewildered passengers had gathered round the light like half-dressed moths. There was incipient panic and it was possible to sense the relief when a ship's officer appeared. He was carrying an electric torch and a board with some papers clipped to it. He seemed to be perfectly calm, apparently trying to convey the impression that everything was completely under control.

'Everyone will please go to their boat stations.'

This announcement was greeted with a babble of inquiry. 'What's happened? Is the ship in danger? Where's the fire? What was all that noise?'

He gestured with the board, and the papers clipped to it fluttered. The top sheet appeared to be a list of names; a boat's muster perhaps.

'There is no cause for alarm,' he said. 'There has been a slight mishap in the engine-room. You will all go to your boat stations as a precautionary measure. But I assure you there is no cause for alarm, none whatever.'

The tilting of the alleyway was a contradiction of his words. In the brief silence that followed they could all hear the crackling of the flames, and the sound appeared to be coming from under their feet.

A voice said: 'No cause for alarm? I'd say there was every cause. The ship's on fire and you know it.'

A woman began to have hysterics.

'If you will all go to your boat stations,' the officer said.

* * *

The shock from the first explosion threw Meade and Helen Tudor to the floor of the cabin. Meade groped in the sudden darkness and his fingers touched the singer's leg.

'What in hell's going on?' he grumbled.

He raised himself to a sitting position. 'Now what do you think that was?'

There was no answer.

'Hey,' he said. 'Have you gone to sleep?'

He put out his hand and touched her again, but she did not move. He pulled the cigarette lighter out of his pocket, flicked it on, and saw that Helen Tudor was lying motionless on her back. There was a smear of blood on her forehead.

He experienced a moment of panic. Suppose she were dead. Suppose he were to be accused of killing her. In the flickering light of the small flame she looked ghastly, corpse-like.

But the moment passed. He saw that she was breathing. She must have struck her head on the edge of the dressing-table as she fell. She was stunned, but she would be all right. There was nothing to worry about.

'Silly bitch,' he muttered. 'Just what you might expect.'

He was trying to rouse her when the second and third explosions rocked the ship, and the floor of the cabin began to tilt. He was not so sure then that there was nothing to worry about. He leaned over the unconscious woman and slapped her face. She did not wake.

Meade was sweating with anxiety. He knew that some disaster had struck the ship; the engines had stopped thumping and the slow, silent shifting of the cabin was frightening.

The tiny flame of the lighter flickered in his hand and he heard someone running past in the alleyway. He shook the woman desperately; she must wake up; she had to; it was imperative that they should get away now, for he felt that the cabin had become a trap. Still she made no movement.

He got to his feet and went to the wash-basin. He found a glass and filled it from the tap. He moved back to the unconscious woman and began to sprinkle water on her face.

'Wake up, can't you? Wake up.'

She opened her eyes at last and stared up at him in bewilderment. 'Arnold! What happened? My head!'

'Never mind your head,' he said savagely. 'You'd better get some clothes on and you'd better be damned quick about it.'

She put a hand to her forehead and sat up, groaning. 'But what's happened? Why has the light gone out? What's wrong with the floor?'

'Everything's wrong. Every damned thing. Don't ask questions; just get some clothes on.'

They could hear people moving in the alleyway, a chatter of excited voices.

Helen seized Meade's arm. 'The ship isn't sinking? It isn't that?'

'How should I know?' He was impatient with her. 'You know as much about that as I do. Why in hell don't you get dressed?'

She got to her feet, swaying. 'Yes, I'd better, hadn't I? She giggled with a trace of hysteria. 'Couldn't go out like this, could I?'

'Get into a shirt and slacks,' Meade said.

'Yes, I'll do that.'

He waited impatiently while she dressed, holding the cigarette lighter like a beacon in his hand. The cabin floor was sloping more acutely and he had to lean against the slope.

Helen said: 'I wish there was more light. I can't see properly. I bet I look terrible.'

'Nobody's going to care a damn what you look like,' Meade said. 'For Pete's sake, hurry.'

40

There was a knock on the door. Someone turned the knob and discovered that the door was locked. A man's voice shouted: 'Anyone in there?'

Meade said softly: 'You'd better open that door.'

She had finished dressing. She went to the door and unlocked it. Meade had moved back behind the door where he could not be seen. He heard the man's voice again.

'Everyone to boat stations, Miss Tudor.'

'What is it?' she asked. 'What's wrong?'

'Just a precaution. But hurry.'

'I'm coming,' she said.

The alleyway was deserted when they left the cabin, and the smoke was thickening. It was like a fog swirling past them; it stung their throats and made their eyes water.

'Arnold, I'm frightened,' Helen said.

He shouted at her angrily: 'Come along, can't you? There's no time to waste.'

He felt certain in his own mind that this call to boat stations was no mere precaution. Before long they would all be in the boats and the ship would be of no more use to them. He went up the alleyway, dragging the woman with him.

★ ★ ★

Barlow and Katherine Summers had been thrown against the rails by the explosion. Barlow's right arm was jarred; it felt numb. He could feel the girl trembling.

'What was it, Chris?'

'I don't know,' he said. 'Are you all right?'

'Yes. Just bruised. It knocked the breath out of me.'

He said: 'I shall have to go and see what's happened. I shall be needed. You know your boat station?'

'Yes,' she said. 'But we shan't be needing the boats, shall we? It isn't as bad as that.'

'I don't expect so,' he said. 'But so long as you know.'

He left her then and was moving towards the bridge when the secondary explosions occurred. They sounded like maroons going off, and a shower of sparks shot up from the funnel and drifted away to starboard. He noticed that the rhythmic tonking of the engine had stopped and that the ship was losing way.

'It's bad,' he muttered. 'It's bad sure enough.'

He broke into a run, still making for the bridge, but before he could get there one of the apprentices almost collided with him. He was in a hurry; he tried to push past Barlow, but the bosun stopped him.

'Somebody on your tail, son?'

The boy said: 'Oh, it's you, bosun. I was on my way to find you.'

'What's the panic?'

'Mr Betts says to muster a fire-fighting party. We can't get any answer from the engine-room on the blower. I think the men down there have been killed. You'd better hurry.'

'I'll hurry,' Barlow said.

He left the apprentice and began to run aft towards the crew's quarters, and as he ran he could feel the ship begin to lean over on her side.

★ ★ ★

Mr King was in his cabin when the explosion came. Neither the sound nor the shock of it seemed to have any effect on him. A person watching him closely would have observed neither astonishment nor dismay portrayed by the bleak, narrow face. It was almost as though he had expected this to happen, had been waiting for it a long time and was satisfied now that it had come.

After the darkness had enveloped him he sat for perhaps a quarter of a minute with his hands gripping the arms of the chair in which he was sitting and his head slightly on one side. He might have been waiting for some call, some summons to action. Perhaps he heard the call inside him, for he got up suddenly, walked across the cabin in the darkness and found a rubber-covered electric torch. He switched it on, found his peaked cap, put the cap on his head and opened a drawer beneath his bunk. From the drawer he took a long-barrelled revolver and two boxes of ammunition. All these he slipped into the pocket of his jacket and then walked to the door and left the cabin.

He had a feeling in his bones that after the lapse of so many barren years he was again very soon to have a command of his own.

★   ★   ★

Two able seamen whose names were respectively Benjamin Fryer and Bartholomew Grimes, an ordinary seaman named Arthur Copley and two greasers, Andrew McKay and Samuel Lynch, had one thing in common: they had all been allotted to the lifeboat which was under the command of the chief officer, Mr Matthew King. This fact might have been of no very great importance if the *Southern Pioneer* had remained afloat, but as things turned out it was to have a considerable effect on the fortunes of several oddly assorted people, an effect that could not possibly have been foreseen when the boat lists had been made out.

Beside these members of the crew, the bosun, and an engineer named Lanyon, the muster roll of Mr King's boat also bore the names of Arnold Meade, Helen

45

Tudor, Stephen Walsh and Katherine Summers. This would have made a round dozen had it not been for Evelyn Partridge, but Miss Partridge was also in the boat, and that brought the complement up to ten men and three women — thirteen souls in all. It was a fact for the superstitious to conjure with if they felt so inclined.

4

A Wide, Wide Sea

The funeral pyre of the *Southern Pioneer* was clearly visible in the night. It was like a torch piercing the darkness, a red tower of flame built on the shifting foundation of the sea, with spires and turrets wavering and flickering as they reached upward, each attempting to outclimb the others and touch with hot fingers the cold faces of the stars.

The four lifeboats lay motionless on the calm sea, and the men and women in the boats watched the death of the ship that so short a while before had been their home. It was too early yet for them to appreciate fully the complete meaning of their loss; it had come upon them so suddenly that there had been no time to think. Now, at a safe distance from the blazing wreck, they sat and watched, all their faces turned to that one point, on all of them the lurid glow of the fire.

In the sternsheets of his boat sat Mr King; he sat straight-backed and rigid like some gaunt carved idol, the deity of that little company of thirteen souls. His face was expressionless; it gave no hint of his feelings, no indication that in this disaster might lie his own triumph, that here in this narrow boat might be the renewal of that command which he had lost when the *Guiding Hand* had struck the reef.

One of the seamen cleared his throat noisily and spat over the gunwale. His spittle made a faint plopping sound as it struck the water, audible even against the background of the sullen roaring of the fire.

'That's one hell of a furnace,' he said. 'Make your eyes sizzle if you was in that little lot. No mistake.'

He rested his hand on the gunwale, thick, scarred fingers ingrained with dirt, his head like brown leather, round and hairless. Benjamin Fryer was a coarse, heavy man in his mid-forties, quick-tempered and violent. Once in Montreal he had killed a man with an empty whisky bottle. It had been a dark night with wind and rain. He had dropped the body in the dock and when it had been fished out there had been nothing to point the finger of suspicion at Ben Fryer two hundred miles away on the high seas.

Other incidents of a similar nature had chequered Fryer's life; he had been in gaols in a dozen different countries; he had had his nose broken in Montevideo, he had lost five teeth in Santiago, his right ear had been half slashed off by a knife in Lagos, and he had had his jaw broken in Buenos Aires.

'Lucky you was watch below, Mac, and you, Sam.' Fryer's voice was hoarse. 'Say it had been your watch on them there engines, you'd be roast pork be now. Same as Charlie and Ginger.'

Andrew McKay and Samuel Lynch shifted uneasily, glancing at Fryer and then looking away again at the red glare of the blazing ship.

'It don't bear thinking on,' Lynch muttered. He had lank, tow-coloured hair, trimmed razor-close as high as the tops of his ears and then left as a kind of rough thatch. On each side of his forehead were deep hollows, as though already the stark contours of a fleshless skull were being delineated. In fact there was about his whole appearance something cadaverous and grave-like, something that seemed to hint of death and corruption.

Andrew McKay, the other greaser, was a small, pale man with a wrinkled skin and quick, bright eyes. He sat huddled on a thwart, sucking his knuckles and saying nothing.

'Charlie and Ginger got theirs all right,' Fryer said. 'No more fun and games for them boys. I bet Charlie sizzled. Fat. He'd melt down like a packet of candles.'

The engineer said in a high, nervous voice: 'Cut it out, Fryer. We don't want any of that talk.'

Fryer turned slowly, mockingly. 'What's the matter, Mr Lanyon? By God, if you'd seen as many ships go up in flames as what I have you wouldn't be crying your eyes out over this one. I've seen men roasted; I've seen 'em burn like ruddy torches, screaming. Tankers, Mr Lanyon, high octane. That was afore your time though. This — ' He waved his hand in the direction of the *Southern Pioneer.* 'This ain't nothing. Why, I could tell you — '

Lanyon said: 'All right, Fryer. That'll be enough. Please remember there are ladies in the boat.'

Wilfred Lanyon was twenty-three and looked younger. He had soft brown eyes and a smooth, almost beardless face. Fryer looked into Lanyon's face, grinning; then he let his glance travel slowly round the boat, allowing it to rest for a moment on each of the three women — on Evelyn Partridge, on Katherine Summers, lastly on Helen Tudor. There it lingered a while.

'Why, so there are, Mr Lanyon, so there are. Much obliged to you for pointing out the fact. I might not have noticed. All the same now, I shouldn't wonder if these here ladies haven't got stomachs that are a sight stronger than yours when it comes to the pinch. It's been my experience that the female of the species is pretty tough. What I say is this — '

It was Mr King's voice that cut in this

time, sharp and incisive as the blade of a knife.

'That will be all from you, Fryer. We have no desire to hear what you would say.'

Fryer turned on the thwart so that he could see the man who had spoken and met the unwavering stare of the chief officer's cold, bleak eyes. It was as though Fryer were seeing him there for the first time, with the lurid glare of the fire lighting him up, and behind him the starry backcloth of the sky and the dark, silent ocean. For a moment Fryer was silent, staring at King; then he gave a laugh.

'Ay, ay, sir. Anything you say. But you know what I been talking about, don't you? You know, Mr King, you know.'

The state of dress, or undress, of the survivors told of the haste with which it had been necessary to abandon ship. Walsh appeared to be the least well prepared for a voyage in an open boat, for he was still wearing his pyjamas and the silk dressing-gown. He sat uncomfortably on one of the centre thwarts with the padded life-jacket about his shoulders and the tapes hanging loose.

He was still frightened. The boat seemed so small a refuge, and the sea was all around them. His tortured mind imagined the boat being overturned, himself drowning, slipping down through layer after layer of cold, dark water. He imagined the monstrous creatures that lived in the depths of the ocean, of sharks and devil-fish, of giant sting-rays and conger eels. He shivered and groaned.

Miss Partridge laid a hand on his arm. 'Are you feeling cold, Mr Walsh?'

He shook her hand away with a petulant gesture. Her calm acceptance of disaster angered him. 'Cold? Of course I'm not cold.'

'I only thought — '

'You thought! What business have you to think? What right — ' He stopped suddenly, realising that hysteria was creeping into his voice, that he was making a fool of himself. He added in a lower tone: 'I'm quite all right, thank you.'

Fryer had been listening to the exchange of words. Fryer was grinning. 'If you're all right I'll lay you're the only one what is.'

Walsh turned on Fryer, his voice snappish. 'Then I am the only one. What's it to you?'

'Gently, gently,' Fryer said, mocking him. 'I only made an observation. No harm in that, is there?'

'Keep your observations to yourself.'

Fryer chuckled but said no more. He rubbed the hard bristle on his chin and stared at the fire.

Able Seaman Bartholomew Grimes and Ordinary Seaman Arthur Copley crouched in the bows of the lifeboat and muttered to each other. Grimes was rat-faced, thin-lipped, ageing. He had served at sea for the greater part of his life and he had been a survivor from four torpedoed ships in the dark days of war. He was not afraid now, but he was angry and bitter.

Grimes had no home but the sea, and all his possessions had been on board the *Southern Pioneer*. Now the sea that he had served had taken the few small, valueless treasures that he had managed to gather around him. In a battered suitcase and a dirty kit-bag they had gone with the ship; with her they would soon be drifting to the bottom of the Pacific Ocean.

'There was that hair-brush I bought in Colombo with the ivory back. I should have saved that.'

Now he was stripped, owning nothing but the clothes he wore and the sheath-knife on his belt.

'I wish I'd kept that hair-brush,' he muttered.

'It was the bosun chasing us,' Copley said. 'Didn't give you no time. Fire party! Where in hell was the use of a fire party in that fire?'

Copley was young and muscular, with black hair that shone with oil. He had a long nose and a hare-lip, and he remembered the war only as a time when you had to give coupons for sweets and spend nights in the Anderson shelter. He had been playing truant from school when Grimes had been clinging to a raft in the North Atlantic. The two men had nothing in common but the bond of a shared fo'c'sle and a shared resentment against authority.

'What do you think our chances are?' Copley said. 'Fifty-fifty?'

'Better, I'd say. Sparks should've got a distress signal away. There'll be ships hunting for us. Planes and all maybe. All we have to do is sit tight and wait for them.'

Copley appeared only half convinced by this reasoning. 'Suppose they don't find us. The sea's an awful big place. Suppose we drift too far. What then?'

Grimes had a secret feeling of contempt for Copley. In his opinion Copley was none too bright; you could split Copley's head open and find nothing but cotton waste and maybe a bit of sawdust mixed in with it.

'There's a wireless transmitter in the Old Man's boat. As long as we keep close to him we're all right.'

'I hope so,' Copley said; but he still did not sound convinced.

★ ★ ★

Katherine Summers could see Barlow's profile outlined against the glare of the fire. She thought it looked clean and strong. She was not afraid; with him there, how could she be afraid? She loved him, and that was all that mattered.

★　★　★

'She's going,' Fryer said softly. 'The old bitch has had it sure enough. She'll do no more sailing.'

The *Southern Pioneer* went down with a hiss. The fire, engulfed by the quenching waters of the Pacific, died like the snuffed-out flame of a candle. Darkness lay upon the water, upon the four boats, and upon the men and women in the boats — darkness and a long silence as they all stared at the point where the ship had been, and now was no more, because the sea had taken her.

5

Cast Off

The beam of an electric torch shone on the boat, falling whitely on the timbers, on the oars lying along the thwarts, on the lashed sail and the thirteen survivors.

'Mr King! Ahoy there! Mr King!'

It was Captain Devons's voice. King turned his head, blinking at the source of the light.

'Sir?'

'I want the boats to stay together, Mr King. To make sure there will be no drifting apart we will pass a line and make fast. You understand?'

'I understand,' King said. 'But I think it's a bad plan nonetheless.'

'I am not asking for your opinion, merely for your cooperation.' Captain Devons's voice was tart. 'Stand by.'

Something came snaking out of the darkness, whipping across the beam of light. It fell athwart the boat and Barlow grabbed it.

'Make fast, bosun,' King said, the words coming out of him as though each had been a good tooth that he was reluctant to part with.

Barlow secured the rope to the bows of the boat. He reported that he had done so.

'Thank you, bosun,' King said with exaggerated politeness. He raised his voice and shouted into the darkness: 'Line secured, Captain Devons.'

Grimes whispered to Copley: 'Don't they love each other, them two. Don't they just.'

'Mr King don't love nobody,' Copley said. 'He's a right bastard.'

A small breeze stirred the water, making it lap gently at the side of the boat. It was the first hint of the possibility of wind. It ruffled Helen Tudor's hair; she could feel it caressing her face like soft fingers. She wondered what she would look like in the morning; a mess no doubt.

She touched Meade's hand in the darkness. 'Arnold.'

'What is it?' He sounded ill-tempered.

'Do we get compensation?'

'Compensation? How do you mean?'

'For the things we've lost. Does the steamship company pay?'

'How should I know? I'm not a lawyer. You were insured, weren't you?'

'Was I? I don't know.'

She let the subject drop. There would be plenty of time to think about that later. For the present the great question was, when would they be picked up? Or even, looking at the blacker side, would they be picked up?

Helen Tudor was afraid. It had become darker. No longer were any stars visible, and though there were lights in the other boats, Mr King had not allowed the lamp in his own boat to be lighted. He had said that they might have need of the oil later and there was only enough for twelve hours. Helen Tudor's imagination began to work, and she pictured in her mind the wind growing to a gale and the ripples becoming gigantic waves that would sweep over the boat and engulf it.

'Arnold,' she whispered. 'Arnold.'

There was no answer this time. She

tried to touch him, but he was no longer sitting on the thwart; he had curled up in the bottom of the boat and was asleep.

★ ★ ★

Some hours passed. The wind had become a little stronger and the cloud had thickened. King was still awake; he rose from the sternsheets and began to make his way to the bows, stepping carefully over the sleeping men and women.

He heard Barlow's voice. 'Who's that?' Barlow spoke softly, as one might in a dormitory.

King answered just as softly: 'Don't disturb yourself, bosun. I'm just taking a look for'ard to make sure that line is all right.'

'It is all right, Mr King,' Barlow said. 'I had a look at it ten minutes ago.'

'No harm in looking again. Why don't you go to sleep? We may have plenty to do in the morning.'

'I don't feel sleepy, sir.'

King left Barlow and found Grimes and Copley snoring in the bows. He could make them out only as a dark heap under the locker. They did not stir.

Still moving softly, he groped and found the rope. He loosed it and began to pay it out over the bows. When he found the end in his hand he leaned over the gunwale and let the rope slide gently into the water, making no splash.

He listened for the sound of a hail from the captain's boat, but none came. No one had noticed the slackening of the rope; no one was aware that one lifeboat was no longer joined to the others, that it was now free — free to make its own way under the command of its master, Matthew King.

He moved back again to the stern, and again heard Barlow's voice.

'Everything in order, sir?'

'Everything, bosun.'

'You think we shall be picked up tomorrow?'

'We are in God's hands, bosun, in God's hands.'

'I think I'll go to sleep now,' Barlow said.

The wind flapped Mr King's jacket and

he heard the sea chuckling. The boat moved uneasily, lifting and falling as the slow waves passed under it. He went back to the stern and waited patiently for the coming of dawn.

★　★　★

A shower of rain woke them to the realization of their perilous situation. One by one they came out of the blessed forgetfulness of sleep and saw the day climbing up over the edge of the sea.

And there were no other boats. They were alone at the centre of a great circle of water, and there was nothing but the sea and the sky and the rain.

Fryer sat up, rubbing the sleep out of his eyes with salty fingers. 'Where they gone to? Where's them others?'

His gaze moved round the horizon. He stood up to widen the radius of his search. He could see no sign of life other than that in the boat beneath his feet. He looked towards the bows and saw that the rope had gone.

'So we come adrift. We come adrift and

63

nobody noticed. Everybody asleep and we come adrift.'

He turned to Barlow. 'You fixed that line; you was supposed to make it fast. And it come adrift. There's bleeding fine seamanship.'

'It was all right when I left it,' Barlow said. 'It was secure enough then.'

'But it ain't now. How d'you explain that? Maybe it worked loose, hey? In the storm. Only there ain't been no storm.'

'It couldn't work loose.'

'Then how come we're adrift?'

'Somebody must have loosed it.'

'That's a likely tale.'

Barlow turned to Mr King for confirmation. 'You had a look at it, sir. You saw it was properly secured. You said so.'

King shook his head. 'I did not say anything of the kind.'

Barlow stared at him in amazement. 'But —'

'I said that everything was in order.'

'Well, then —'

'The two things are not quite the same. I might have added, if I had been so minded, that I had cast off the shackles of

Captain Devons's authority.'

Barlow was bewildered. 'I don't understand, sir.'

'To put it plainly, it was I who cast us adrift. I loosed the rope. That was my purpose in going for'ard when you spoke to me. My sole purpose.'

They were all staring at him now. He sat in the sternsheets, upright, stiff, forbidding, his sharp jaw thrust forward, his lips pressed together in a hard, thin line.

He spoke again after a brief pause. 'Does anyone wish to question my action?'

Barlow said slowly, shaking his head: 'But where's the point? The radio is in the captain's boat. We were supposed to stay close. Those were the orders. Captain Devons said — '

King broke in sharply: 'I take no orders from Devons. I take orders from no one. I give them. You understand?'

Walsh cleared his throat noisily and began to speak. 'Are we to understand that on your own authority you have deliberately caused this boat to become separated from the others?'

'That is so, Mr Walsh.'

'To what purpose?'

King made no answer for a few moments. Then he said: 'It is essential before we proceed any further that you should understand here and now that I do not feel called upon to explain or excuse any action that I may decide to take. I trust you are satisfied, Mr Walsh.'

Walsh exploded suddenly under the pricking of fear and anger. 'No, sir, I am not satisfied. I am very far from satisfied. For God's sake, man, don't you realize you're gambling with the lives of all of us in this boat?'

'Thirteen lives,' Grimes muttered, pulling at his lower lip. 'Thirteen unfortunates.'

Walsh swept on. 'Don't you realize you are placing us all in jeopardy?'

'You were in jeopardy already,' King said. 'I do not consider that any action of mine has increased the danger.'

'You do not consider! Well, that's all very fine, but perhaps some of us have a different opinion. The captain said we were to stick together. He must have thought that was the best chance we had of being saved.'

'I have no doubt at all that that was what he thought.'

'And wasn't he right?'

'That is a matter of opinion.'

'It is not yours?'

'Mr Walsh,' King said, 'I will tell you something. I will tell all of you, so that there can be no mistake. My idea of salvation is not to wait passively for help to drop from the sky. I am not an Israelite wandering in the wilderness and being fed with manna from heaven. I am a man of action; I believe in striving actively for what I desire. The prizes of this life are not thrust into one's hand; they have to be reached for and grasped firmly or they will slip away for ever. That is why I have cast this boat adrift from the others.'

'Then you have disobeyed your captain's orders.'

'I have no captain but myself. Since this boat was launched I, and I alone, have been her captain. This boat is under my command and it is I who make all decisions. Mine is the sole responsibility, and anyone who disobeys my orders is guilty of insubordination.'

There was a brief silence in the boat. They could hear the rain pattering on the timbers and the sea lapping against the sides. They all stared at King, turning his words over in their minds and considering how this might affect each one of them.

Barlow was the first to break the silence. He said: 'Are we allowed to ask what your plans are, sir?'

King nodded. 'Certainly you are. We are about to set out on a voyage of discovery.'

'Where to, sir?'

'That remains to be seen. As I have said, it will be a voyage of discovery. A great deal may be discovered. The sea is vast and there are many islands. Who can tell what it may hold for us?'

Meade whispered to Helen Tudor: 'I don't like this. I believe that man's off his head. He's cracked. You can see it in his eyes.'

Fryer began to laugh, his great stomach quivering with the laughter. 'You're a one, Mr King, truth you are. You're a lad and no mistake.'

'I did not ask for any comment from you,' King said flintily. 'Your opinion is of no consequence whatever.'

Fryer stopped laughing suddenly and his face became evil. 'Maybe you get what you don't ask for, and then again maybe you don't get what you do ask for. There's some of us don't go a lot on that voyage of discovery lark. We think we'd rather join up with them other boats. What you say, boys?'

He turned to the other seamen and the two greasers, and there was a murmur of agreement. It was apparent that Fryer was their leader. He nodded his bald head with satisfaction and his thick neck bulged.

'You heard that, Mr King? We want to go back.'

King gave no indication that he had heard Fryer. He spoke with icy calm. 'Bosun, you will see to the stepping of the mast and rigging of the sail. At once.'

Barlow hesitated. He did not know what King's purpose was, but he believed that this course of action was utterly misguided. Within a few days at most there would be rescue ships at the spot where the *Southern Pioneer* had gone down, and it was there that their best hope of survival lay. Yet King was proposing to sail away from that position, to sail away in an open boat to God knew where. It was madness.

'I am waiting, bosun,' King said.

'Are you sure you're doing the right thing, sir? Don't you think Fryer is right? This is taking an almighty risk.'

'Hoist the sail, bosun.'

Barlow shrugged. An order was an order, and King was in command. 'All right, lads. Unlash the sail.'

'Not me,' Fryer said. 'I ain't touching it. I say we better find them other boats.'

Barlow looked at Copley and Grimes. They had not moved from their position in the bows.

Fryer said to them: 'What about you two? You want to commit harry-karry for Mr King?'

They shook their heads dumbly. Grimes's eyes were watchful and beady. Copley's tongue came out and licked at his hare-lip. But they made no move to

70

carry out orders; they had become accustomed to following Fryer's lead in the fo'c'sle and they were following it now.

Since Walsh had had his say the passengers had been silent. They were bewildered, not knowing whether King was in the right or the men who were defying him. Lanyon, the young engineer, was nervously biting his finger-nails and wishing that he had had the good fortune to be allotted to one of the other boats. He did not care for the look of things in this one.

King's voice cut the silence like acid biting into metal. 'Are you disobeying orders, Fryer?'

'You could maybe call it that,' Fryer said, staring at King from under his bunched eyebrows.

Sam Lynch muttered hoarsely: 'Ben's right. Ben knows what's what.'

McKay also nodded approval. 'Ay, he is that.'

There were five men in the boat undoubtedly opposed to King, and it was apparent that the sympathies of the

71

passengers were with them. Lanyon and Barlow, if it came to the push, would support King, not because they thought he was right but because they felt it was their duty to do so. But they did not like it.

King's voice hardened. 'I am giving you a last chance, Fryer. Are you going to obey orders Yes or no?'

'No,' Fryer shouted. 'No, and be damned to you.'

'Very well,' King said. 'I see that I shall have to resort to coercion.' He put his right hand in the pocket of his jacket and pulled out the revolver. He pointed it at Fryer and the barrel did not waver. 'Possibly this will persuade you.'

Fryer looked at the revolver and made no move. 'Kids' games, Mr King,' he said contemptuously. 'You better put that thing away before it goes off. You might hurt yourself.'

The revolver barked suddenly and a splinter of wood was ripped off the gunwale two inches from where Fryer's hand was resting. Fryer's mouth sagged open and he stared at the furrow that the bullet had gouged.

King said crisply: 'Now, bosun, let's have that sail hoisted and no more nonsense.'

Fryer looked at King with a kind of awed wonder. The colour had drained away from his lips and he was licking them with his thick, coarse tongue.

'By Christ,' he muttered, 'the bastard is mad. He is mad and no mistake.'

He moved to help the others with the mast and sail, still watching King warily out of the corners of his eyes.

Barlow noticed that Fryer's hands were shaking. It looked as though Mr King meant to be master in his own boat. Yes, it certainly looked that way.

6

Voyage

The lifeboat moved slowly over a calm sea. The water glittered under the sun and the occupants of the boat sweltered in the heat.

Five days had passed since the loss of the *Southern Pioner* and in those five days they had seen no ship, no other boat, no land.

At first it had been in Fryer's mind to take the revolver from King by stealth during the night and force him to return to their original position. But King never appeared to sleep and he seemed to be endowed with the eyes of a cat. However silently Fryer might creep up on him it was only to be met with the cool inquiry: 'Is that you, Fryer? What are you up to, man?'

Mr King was not to be taken by surprise.

After two days Fryer gave up the idea. It was too late. They were in King's hands and there was no going back.

Having accepted this fact, Fryer looked around him and decided that there might be compensations. He let his gaze rest on Helen Tudor and licked his thick lips. Now and then he chuckled softly to himself.

It was the sun that was their greatest enemy; it scorched and tormented them, burning their skins and producing thirsts that the strict ration of water was insufficient to satisfy The surface of the sea, rippled by a gentle wind, was a mirror from whose countless faces the sun's rays were flung back like glittering spears to probe and torture the eyes of the survivors in the boat.

Night came as a relief. Then they might sleep and dream that all this was past, that they were no longer in an open boat in the midst of a great expanse of ocean, but once more on dry land, able to walk in the shade and drink from cool fountains, to drink and drink.

It was from such a dream as this that

Helen Tudor awoke in the middle of the fifth night. She could feel a hand touching her, fumbling, searching.

She was still only half awake. She murmured sleepily: 'Arnold. Darling.'

She heard a man chuckle throatily close to her ear. Suddenly she was wide awake and she knew that the man was not Arnold Meade. She started to scream, but almost before a sound could leave her throat the hand shifted to her mouth, gagging her.

'Stow it, you silly bitch,' Fryer hissed. 'Quiet, damn you.'

She could smell his hand under her nose and the taste of it was in her mouth; her lips were being crushed against her teeth with cruel pressure. The coarse bristle of Fryer's chin scraped her cheek like a rasp. There was a reek of sweat about him and his breath was repellent. She felt sick and frightened.

'Don't pretend you don't like it,' Fryer whispered. 'I know your sort.'

He still kept one hand on her mouth, but the other now began to pull at her clothing. She felt the night air suddenly cold on her bare skin. Fryer's breathing quickened, whistling through his nostrils as if under pressure.

She trembled with disgust and struggled to free herself, but Fryer was a powerful man and his weight was on her, crushing her into the bottom of the boat. She could feel the hard timbers pressing into her back.

'Stop wriggling. What's up with you?' He was keeping his voice low, but it was tense with excitement. 'Come on now. You've put up enough show. Come on.'

She felt the strength draining out of her. Above her the stars seemed to be revolving like a kaleidoscope, a mad cascade of flickering points of light.'

Fryer sensed her weakness, the slackening of resistance. 'That's better, sweetheart. Now you're being sensible. Just stay quiet like a good girl.'

Then suddenly there was another voice, which she recognized as the bosun's. 'You damned bastard.'

The weight of Fryer's body was lifted from her and she heard a thudding sound such as a fist might make striking flesh.

Dark, confused shapes moved above Helen Tudor; she could hear the men's laboured breathing as they struggled. Any moment it seemed that one or both of them might fall out of the boat; there was no room for fighting in that confined space.

It was Mr King who put a stop to the business. 'What the devil is going on there?'

The beam of an electric torch shone through the darkness and threw its light on the two struggling men and the woman lying at their feet.

'What is all this?' King demanded. 'Bosun, what in blazes are you trying to do?'

Barlow dropped his hands and stood away from Fryer. 'You'd better ask him what he was trying to do.'

Fryer rubbed his jaw and said nothing. King spoke again, testily: 'Well, Fryer, let's have it. What have you got to say for yourself?'

'The bosun hit me,' Fryer said. 'You know that ain't legal, sir. He ain't allowed to hit a man.'

'Why did you hit him, bosun?'

'Let him tell you.'

'I'm asking you.'

Helen Tudor was sitting up. She pointed at Fryer accusingly. 'That man assaulted me.'

'Is that so, Fryer?' King's voice was cold, but there was anger in it.

Fryer said sneeringly: 'I kissed her, that's all. She liked it; she liked it well enough. Now she's kicking up a stink just for the look of things.' He stabbed a finger at Barlow. 'If he hadn't come poking his snout in there wouldn't have been no trouble.'

Barlow made a movement towards Fryer, but King's voice halted him. 'No more of that, bosun. I'll have no brawling in this boat.' He turned to Fryer and his voice rasped. 'As for you, in future you will keep away from the women. If you so much as touch one of them with your little finger, by God I'll put a bullet through your head. Do you understand?'

'I understand,' Fryer said sulkily.

'Remember it then.'

The torch was switched off; the night

closed in on them again; but it was a long while before any of the thirteen survivors of the *Southern Pioneer* went back to sleep.

* * *

Day came, and it was like the other days, with the hot sun and the jewelled sea, the heat and the thirst and the discomfort. Miss Partridge, prim, tidy, unruffled, helped to measure out the rations, dispensed ointment from the medical box for sunburn, and encouraged Katherine Summers with cheerful words.

'It will soon be over. We shall be picked up or we shall reach land. One or the other.'

Mr King was the navigator. He set the course and accepted no argument. They were all in his hands now; if any man was to get them to land, he was that man; none of the others was capable of navigation. He revealed nothing of his plans, took no one into his confidence. He was the master, and the master did not confide in subordinates.

When Walsh asked: 'Where are we heading?' King answered briefly: 'That you will discover in due course.'

Walsh was annoyed. He was not accustomed to being treated as a small boy. 'But really, Mr King, we have a right to some information.'

'I recognize no such right.'

Walsh spluttered. He was a slightly ridiculous figure in his striped pyjamas, his waist not yet reduced to a healthy size by the rigour of the boat's diet. The stubble was black on his sagging face and his hair was uncombed.

'You can't treat us like this. It's disgraceful. I demand to know our destination.'

King was unmoved. 'It could be heaven, Mr Walsh. It could conceivably be hell.'

Walsh's chin quivered. 'I must inform you that I have an important manufacturing business that I need to keep in touch with. How can I tell what's going on? Anything might be happening — anything.'

He felt cut off now more than ever. Now there was no possibility whatever of getting a message through to Jackson. He had lost control. Goodness only knew what that reckless young man might do in his absence.

'I should never have come,' he muttered. 'It was a mad thing to do.'

Arnold Meade had become philosophical about the situation. He was not afraid, since he did not believe that the boat was in any great danger. King probably knew what he was doing, even though he had taken upon himself the role of a god. And afterwards it might be good publicity. He imagined the headlines: 'Tennis star in thrilling drama of the sea. Arnold Meade takes to the boats.' Publicity could help a lot.

Meade's beard was golden and his hair was like spun metal, the kind that neither wind nor rain could disorder. His skin had already been so deeply tanned that the sun had no power to burn it, and he looked virile, muscular and handsome. He might have been a Greek prince bound for the siege of Troy; he could have stood for a model of Achilles.

Mr King regarded him with some

distaste, making little effort to disguise the contempt he felt for a man who went round the world doing nothing more productive than playing tennis. In King's opinion Meade was not pulling his weight; a man ought to work for his living, and knocking a ball over a net with a racket could not be called work.

★　★　★

Ten days had passed since the *Southern Pioneer* had gone down. There was a smell of paint and tar, of stale sweat and wet timber. They trailed their fingers in the sea and washed themselves in salt water. Cracks opened in their skin and refused to heal; the darker men were tanned to the colour of old mahogany and there were wrinkles around their eyes caused by much squinting in the glaring light.

The shadow of the sail lay on the surface of the water like a cape; it shrank as the sun climbed the sky and grew again as the sun declined; it was a measure of the slow and tedious passage of time.

Their beards grew longer and the supply of fresh water dribbled away.

It was Grimes who accused Miss Partridge of favouritism in doling out the precious liquid. 'She gives them more than us.' In his accusation he divided the lifeboat into two camps: Walsh, Meade, Lanyon, Barlow, the three women and King on one side, the five seamen on the other. It was a class distinction in this miniature world of a ship's boat.

'I seen her dipping it out,' Grimes said. 'I watched her. I want my fair share.'

'I have no favourites,' Miss Partridge said crisply. 'We all share alike.'

'Damn that for a tale. I got eyes, ain't I?'

'If you have eyes you should be able to see that no one gets more than another.'

'What about nights?' Grimes said. 'Who's to say you don't dish out a bit extra for the lucky ones when we're asleep?'

His thin, wizened faced was screwed up into an expression of venom; his beard had grown only in patches like a sparse crop of corn on bad land. Miss Partridge regarded him with contempt.

'You are being offensive. But I suppose that is only to be expected from one of your sort.'

'My sort! What do you mean by that, hey? What's my sort? Come on now, let's have it straight.'

'Only a person with a small, warped mind would suspect what you have accused me of doing.'

'Small, warped mind, is it now?' Grimes's voice had become shrill. He was working himself up into a rage. 'I don't have to listen to insults from an old bitch like you. I don't — '

King cut him short. 'That will be enough, Grimes. I'll have no more of these wild accusations. I have complete confidence in Miss Partridge's impartiality. You have as much water as any of us.'

Grimes muttered something under his breath and King barked at him: 'What was that? Speak up, man. If you have anything to say, say it loud enough for all of us to hear. Well, have you?'

Grimes stared at King for a moment, but his glance wavered and dropped before the steely glare of King's eyes.

'Nothing to say.'

'Very well,' King said. 'Let it stay that way.'

* * *

It was two nights later when Meade caught Grimes helping himself to the water. Meade happened to be awake and heard the rattle of the dipper; and he was all the more enraged because of the torment of his own thirst. He struck Grimes with his clenched fist, and he struck hard. Grimes rolled in the bottom of the boat, cursing. But in a moment he had whipped out his knife and had opened a long gash in Meade's forearm. Meade's yell of pain roused the others.

'That little rat,' Meade shouted. 'He was stealing the water and he knifed me. I'll break his neck.'

'You keep off me,' Grimes snarled. 'Else you may get it in a worse place.'

He stood with the knife gripped in his hand, waiting for Meade, and that was how the beam of King's torch revealed

86

them, showing the blood oozing from a shallow gash in Meade's arm.

Grimes slipped the knife back in its sheath. He looked scared but defiant. He even made an attempt to shift the blame on to Meade.

'You don't want to believe him. It was him what was at the water. I caught him at it and he hit me on the jaw.'

Meade was taken aback by such brazen lying. 'Why, you little swine. So that's your story. Do you think anybody is going to believe that?'

'I don't care if they believe it or not,' Grimes snarled. He blinked into the light of the torch. 'And that goes for you too, Mr Almighty King. I ain't going to be sat on no more. I know my rights.'

'Bartholomew Grimes,' King said. 'Can you give me one good reason why I should not shoot you between the eyes and throw your wretched carcase overboard?'

Grimes began to stutter. The revolver was in King's right hand and there was no hint of mercy in his voice.

'I never done nothing,' Grimes screamed. 'It was him, I tell you. It was him.'

Fryer interposed in his harsh, grating voice: 'He's right, Mr King. You can't condemn a man out of hand. It's only Mr Meade's word against his.'

'Keep out of this, Fryer,' King said. He stepped over a thwart and brought himself close to Grimes. The revolver barrel went up and came down. There was a thud clearly audible in the hushed boat. Grimes fell forward and lay across the thwart, a dark smear of blood on his forehead.

Mr King returned to the sternsheets and sat down. Once again he had demonstrated where authority lay.

★　★　★

The boat sailed on into the next day and Meade sat with a bandage on his left arm. There was a dark bruise and congealed blood on Grimes's forehead, and when he looked at Meade's handsome face and golden hair there was venom in his eyes.

7

Land

It appeared to the south-west of them. It was like a cloud lying on the water very far off; it had no clear-cut lines, no hardness; it could have been a mirage, something that the imagination had conjured out of hope and longing; a dream, an hallucination, a bank of mist.

But the seamen were not deceived; they knew that it was land.

'You see, Mr Walsh,' Barlow said. 'We are not going to die after all.'

'I can't believe it,' Walsh said. 'It doesn't look solid.'

'But it is — as you will see.'

It was early morning; the sun had scarcely risen and the freshness of night had not completely gone from the air. Soon again it would be hot, almost unbearably so. But soon too they might be ashore, perhaps under the shade of trees, hard ground under their feet.

Fryer licked his dry lips and his eyes glamed. He took off the sweaty, salt-caked woollen cap that he had been wearing, revealing the polished brown skin of his head. He waved the cap in exultation.

'By God, it's good to see it. I got the cramp in my bones from sitting in this boat. I want to stretch my legs and walk about.'

'We ain't there yet,' Grimes said sourly.

Fryer slapped him on the shoulder. 'But we shall be, shipmate. We shall be.'

'How do we get there?' Grimes asked. 'Not enough wind to lift a feather.'

The sail hung limply from the mast, and if there was any movement of the boat it was so small as to be unnoticeable. There was no steerage way and the rudder was a useless slab of timber hanging at the stern.

'You better whistle for a wind,' Grimes said.

Mr King was a silent, motionless figure in the sternsheets, his peaked cap on his head, his bony face almost black from exposure to the sun and wind. There was no hint of triumph in his expression, but he had said they would reach land, and the land was there.

They heard the sudden bark of his orders: 'Lower the sail. Man the oars.'

'Ay, ay, sir.'

There was no hesitation now, no questioning of the command. The land was calling to them. If they had heard the Sirens singing they could not have been more irresistibly drawn to that faint, misty line on the horizon, they would not more willingly have thrust the oar-blades into the sparkling sea.

They used four oars on each side, Meade taking one as well as the seamen and the engineer. Even Walsh, in the first flush of enthusiasm, lent his weight to Grimes's oar. But Walsh was soon gasping for breath and the rough timber of the oar rasped his soft hands. He glanced over his shoulder, expecting the land to be looming up, clear and solid, after so much effort, but he could detect hardly any alteration in the appearance of that goal for which they were steering. He groaned and heard Grimes's voice jerking out the words in time with the rhythm of his rowing.

'What's up? Can't you take it, hey?'

'I'm done for,' Walsh said. 'I can't go on any longer. Back, hands — done for.'

He dropped his hands from the oar and sat on the thwart with his arms slack at his sides, his shoulders hunched, his face dripping with sweat.

Grimes glanced at him contemptuously. 'Soft as a jelly. Never done a day's work. Soft.'

Meade was feeling the strain also, but he would not give in. He was an athlete and had a pride in his own fitness. So he kept at it while his hands blistered and his shoulders ached; but he was thankful when King gave the order to rest.

King spoke to Miss Partridge. 'Give the men a ration of water.'

Meade kept the water in his mouth for a long while before swallowing. He could have drunk a gallon, and the wretchedly small quantity that was doled out served only to tantalise with its promise of what a real drink would taste like. When it had gone his mouth felt as dry as ever.

'We made a bit of distance,' Fryer said. 'The way some cripples was rowing, it's a wonder we shifted at all.' He looked meaningly at Walsh and Meade. Walsh was not listening and Meade ignored the remark.

The land was more clearly visible now, and it seemed to stretch for a great distance. It was no small coral island but a real landfall. They could see the outline of green mountains.

'Man the oars,' King said.

They bent again to the labour; again the boat moved sluggishly forward like a heavy wagon axle-deep in mud. In the toil and sweat of the rowers the land came nearer, and the lean man who steered the boat watched with his cold eyes the approach of that world, that kingdom, to attain which he had cut adrift from the other boats, preferring to strike out on an independent course that might bring him again to the power he had lost so many years ago. Or even to a greater power than that.

The white line of the shore became clearer where the waves broke in foam.

Away to port was a high cliff dropping sheer to the water's edge; and to starboard, perhaps a mile or so distant, was another similar cliff. Between the two cliffs, sheltered and isolated by them, was a curving beach.

'It's not simply a coral island,' Miss Partridge said to Katherine Summers. 'I've seen coral islands and atolls. This must be a very big island.'

Katherine Summers shaded her eyes with her hand and looked towards the beach. Here and there were clumps of palm trees growing almost to the edge of the sea; beyond them the steeply rising land, the mountains.

'Do you suppose there are savages?'

Miss Partridge smiled at the notion. 'All savages are civilized now — more or less. None of them any longer indulge in cannibalism or head-hunting.'

'How do you know?'

'I have been told so.'

Katherine Summers appeared to be only partly convinced by this assurance. She continued to stare at the land, searching for any indication of human life, any painted warriors dancing on the beach and waving spears. She could see nothing of the kind; the land seemed utterly peaceful; the sun flamed down upon it and nothing moved. But beyond the beach it was dark and secret; it might have been watching them, waiting for them to disturb the settled rhythm of its existence.

'I don't like it,' Katherine said. 'It makes me afraid.'

She could not have explained why she should have been afraid; it was a vague uneasiness, perhaps a presentiment of evil. There was no logical basis for it, but it was there.

Miss Partridge patted her hand. 'There's no need to be. We're safe now. The danger is all behind us.'

'All?'

'Of course.'

Helen Tudor listened to the grunting of the rowers, to the splash of the oars and the creaking of the rowlocks. She saw the sweat gleaming on the men's faces and dripping into the stubble of their chins; she saw the muscles swelling in their arms and the corded sinews. These were the animals on whom her life depended. She looked away from them at the oarblades; she watched the silver drops of water flung from the blades as they swept forward to dip and thrust again.

Ahead was the land and freedom from the dangers of the sea, but who could tell what other dangers might be lying in wait for them? She looked again at the rowers and caught Fryer's eye. When he saw her watching him he leered and winked. She turned away, but she could hear him chuckling; and the sound of that chuckle was an obscenity in itself; it might have been an echo of the thoughts in Fryer's mind.

The sound of the breakers on the beach came to them as they crept nearer; they could hear the murmur of the surf; it made a background to the creaking of the oars.

'Nearly there, boys,' Barlow said.

'And need to be,' Lynch grumbled. 'We bin at these bleedin' oars long enough to row to Australia.'

'You engine-room softies,' Fryer mocked.

'What's the matter with you? Look at Mr Meade there, doing his whack and no grumbles. And him one of the bloomin' aristocrats what's paid his fare.'

Meade's hands were sore, but he would not give in, not in front of these seamen, not in front of the women. If nothing else could have kept him going, his vanity would. There was blood on his blistered palms, but he gritted his teeth and kept at it to the end.

King avoided the high, sheer cliff on the port side and steered for the beach. He could see a few jagged rocks thrusting up from the water and breaking it into a swirl of foam, but if he avoided them also it seemed that there was nothing to stop the boat from reaching the smooth sand of the beach.

'No more trouble now, mates,' Fryer said. 'Home and dry.'

He had exulted a little too soon. The boat was lifted on a wave, drove forward and came down with a rush. There was a grinding, splintering sound that put fear into Walsh's heart. The sharp point of a rock like the pinnacle of a submerged

97

steeple came up through the bottom and the boat stopped dead.

They were only a few yards from the beach, but they were not quite home and dry. Water was welling up through the hole in the bottom and a wave splashed more water over the gunwale.

Helen Tudor gave a scream.

'Stop that,' King said sharply. He seemed unmoved by this cruel stroke of fortune. 'How deep is it, bosun?'

Barlow sounded with an oar and found that the rock was an isolated projection. He could not reach bottom.

'I could take a line ashore,' Barlow said. 'We could haul the non-swimmers in life-jackets.'

'Do that,' King said.

Barlow picked up the rope and tied it about his waist. He stepped over the gunwale and began to swim strongly towards the beach with Fryer paying out the rope behind him. He felt the sand under his feet and staggered forward through the surf and up on to the beach, the first of the survivors to reach the land.

He held the end of the rope while the

others came along it hand over hand. Within a few minutes they were all ashore, their wet clothes clinging to them, the salt water drying quickly from their faces.

'We've lost the boat,' Fryer said. 'No more sea voyages for her. It's the land for us now.'

'And a good thing too,' Lynch said. 'To hell with the sea.'

Fryer turned and stared at the green wall of vegetation that was like a screen enclosing the secrets of this land to which they had come, and there was a trace of uneasiness in his voice. 'I wonder what's back there. I wonder.'

There was no sound but the low thunder of the surf as the waves rolled up the beach.

'I wonder,' Fryer said again. 'I wonder.'

He walked a short distance up the beach and saw an object lying, half-buried, in the sand. He dug it out with his foot and picked it up. He held it aloft in his hand and turned to exhibit it to the others.

'See,' he shouted. 'We got somebody to welcome us.'

They all stared at him, at the thing he held in his hand. It was a human skull.

'But he ain't talking,' Fryer said. 'He ain't saying a word.'

With a sudden movement he flung the skull away from him. It travelled in a shallow arc and came to rest in the sand.

'There's manners for you,' Grimes said. 'He ain't been here two ticks and he starts throwing the host around. Or maybe the hostess. Shameful.'

The skull lay on the wet sand and the surf came washing up around it. When the sea retreated a coating of foam was left clinging to the skull. It looked like a ragged fringe of hair, white as death.

8

Seat of Judgement

Barlow could see Katherine in the distance as he came back along the beach. She was standing at the edge of the sea, letting the water swill about her ankles. She was perfectly motionless, and so intent on watching the horizon that she did not hear Barlow until he was close to her.

'What can you see?' he asked. 'A ship?'

She turned quickly. Her arms, her legs and her face were dyed brown by the sun, and to Barlow it seemed that exposure to the elements suited her. She looked more spirited, more alive than she had ever seemed on board the *Southern Pioneer*.

'It's nothing,' she said. 'I thought there was a wisp of smoke, but it was nothing.'

'Did you want it to be a ship? Do you want to get away from here?'

She seemed to give the question some

101

thought before answering: 'I really don't know if that is what I want.'

'But you wouldn't like to stay here for ever?'

'No, not for ever. Not without any hope of getting away. But perhaps for a time. If only — '

'If only what?'

'If only I were not afraid.'

Barlow stirred the sand with his toes. He was leaner than he had been; there seemed to be no flesh anywhere on his body that was not tough and sinewy.

'Afraid of what?'

Her answer surprised him; it was not what he had expected. 'Of Mr King.'

He said: 'There's no need to be afraid of him. He's harmless.'

'Oh,' she said, 'I'm not afraid of him physically, not in the way I might be afraid of Fryer. But Mr King is more dangerous, I think, than any of the others.'

'I don't understand. In what way is he dangerous?'

'He's not normal, is he?'

'Maybe a little eccentric,' Barlow admitted reluctantly. 'But who isn't?'

'I believe it's more than eccentricity. He has an obsession.'

'What kind of obsession?'

'Power. I think he has some mad desire to have absolute authority over us.'

'Somebody has to make the rules and see that they're carried out. Otherwise there might be anarchy. There are some tough boys here; if it were not for Mr King's revolver they could get out of hand. You should be glad he is here.'

'I know. But all the same — '

'You think he's playing the despot a shade too much? Perhaps he is, but I shouldn't let it worry you. Better him than Fryer or Grimes or Lynch.'

They began to walk towards the north cliff in which they had discovered caves on the first day. On their right were the palms, and beyond the palms the jungle and the mountains, the unknown interior.

'Tomorrow,' Barlow said. 'Wilf Lanyon and I are going inland.'

'I wish you weren't going,' she said.

'It's only for a while. Somebody's got to go. No good simply waiting on this beach and hoping to be picked up by a passing ship.'

'It was a pity the boat was smashed.'

A storm had blown up on the third day and under the battering of the waves the boat had broken up. Fortunately, they had already carried most of the gear and stores ashore — the oars and canvas, a boat-hook, the medical chest, a tin of biscuits, four tins of corned beef, fishing-tackle, a hatchet, two water breakers, some lengths of rope and cord.

They were in no danger of starvation; there were shell-fish and other fish for the catching; there were coconuts and fruit to be gathered; and about half a mile south of the place where they had come ashore they discovered a fresh-water stream. Following this stream back a short way inland they had found a rocky pool fed by a waterfall cascading from a height.

They had established themselves in the caves. King had allotted one cave to the women, one to the men, and a third to himself. He seemed to have become even more aloof, even more taciturn and reserved than he had been in the boat. He gave orders, but he discussed nothing with the others; it was as though he considered them too far beneath him to be worthy of his conversation.

There was evidence that the caves had been occupied before; crude drawings had been scratched on the walls and there were more skulls like the one they had found on the beach. Fryer, for whom skulls seemed to have a fascination, took one of them out into the sunlight, balancing it on the palm of his hand.

'There's one joker that's been taken off the ration list. Good teeth and all. Wasted on him.'

The skull made Helen Tudor feel sick. She turned away in disgust. 'It's horrible.'

Fryer leered at her. 'Wouldn't you like it for an ornament? Nice thing to have around the house. Lend a bit of class without being noisy.' He tossed the skull towards her and it fell at her feet, grinning up at her. She shuddered and walked away from it. Fryer laughed.

For King also the skulls seemed to have some strange appeal. He had them brought out of the cave and set up on stakes in a semi-circle. He offered no reason; he merely gave the order and watched as it was carried out.

'He's cracked,' Grimes said to Copley. 'He's been too long in the sun. But why worry? A few skulls never done nobody any harm.'

When the wind blew in off the sea it made a hollow whistling sound in the grove of skulls. It was as though they had found again some of that breath which had gone out of them for the last time so long ago.

As Barlow and Katherine approached they saw the grinning semi-circle.

'Those things send shivers up my spine,' Katherine said. 'Why did he have them set up like that?'

'Who knows? A whim.'

'Is that another whim?'

She pointed, and Barlow saw Lynch and Grimes carrying a roughly constructed chair. The two men set it down within the semi-circle of skulls and stood back as if to admire their handiwork. The other survivors gathered round.

'Behold the throne,' Grimes said.

'There's a pretty bit of joinery for you.'

Lanyon detached himself from the group and walked to meet Barlow and Katherine. He looked worried.

'So they've finished making the chair,' Barlow said. 'Why have they put it there?'

'Mr King's orders.'

'It's a queer idea.'

'King's ideas are queer,' Lanyon said. 'And they get queerer. To tell the truth, I don't like the way things are going here.'

Barlow said reassuringly: 'Things are going fine. We're lucky to be alive. We've got food and shelter. We could be a lot worse off.'

'We've got a dictator too.'

'Mr King? He's only concerned with the welfare of the colony.'

'Colony? It's more like an independent state. Do you know what he's calling that chair? The Seat of Judgement. In future anyone who has a request or a complaint to make has got to bring it one hour before sundown when King will be sitting there to hear it.'

Barlow looked into Lanyon's eyes. The engineer was scared; there could be no doubt about that.

'You think he's mad, don't you?'

'Yes,' Lanyon said. 'I do.'

'It may not be as bad as that. Perhaps it's just a desire for power and all the trappings. He used to be a ship's captain, you know. He's had to take orders from younger men for a long time and it must have been galling. This could be some kind of reaction.'

'Other men have had a desire for power. Hitler and Mussolini.'

'But King isn't like them. He isn't doing anything bad. If he has these little ideas of play-acting we've just got to humour him. It doesn't hurt us.'

Lanyon shook his head gloomily. 'Not yet perhaps. But he may go too far.'

'If he does we can stop him.'

'He's got the gun. He wouldn't be afraid to use it.'

'He couldn't do much against nine other men even with a revolver. He'd have to see sense.'

'Lunatics don't see sense.' Lanyon glanced at the group gathered round the chair. He lowered his voice. 'Besides, how

108

would you feel about lining yourself up with that lot? Meade and Walsh may be all right, but what about Fryer and Lynch and Grimes? What about McKay and Copley? How would you like to be stuck with that crew?'

'I wouldn't like it,' Barlow admitted. 'Copley perhaps excepted, they're as fine a set of bilge dredgings as you'd find.'

'We've got the scum of the *Southern Pioneer's* crew here. We were dead unlucky to be in that particular boat. Mr King and that lot; it couldn't have been worse.'

Katherine said softly: 'Scum rises to the top.'

Lanyon nodded. 'That's why we need Mr King. It's not pleasant to have to depend on a man who's got a screw loose, but that's how it is.'

'It may not be quite as bad as you've painted it,' Barlow said. 'I think you're letting your imagination run away with you. Anyway, tomorrow we're going on a journey of discovery.'

'I didn't think he was going to let us go.'

'He seemed to be in two minds, but he

has allowed it, so that's that.'

'Here comes Mr King,' Katherine said.

King looked as gaunt as a rock. His shirt and trousers were stained with salt and his beard was streaked with grey. He carried the revolver in his belt and he walked stiffly, as one might have expected a skeleton to walk; you could almost fancy you heard the bones creaking.

Everybody looked at him and he looked at no one; his gaze passed over them or through them; they might have been invisible.

'You see that,' Lanyon whispered. 'It's as if he regarded us as dirt, not good enough to lick his shoes.'

Grimes made way for King, nodding and smirking. 'Here you are, sir. Here's your lordship's chair all ready and waiting like you ordered.'

He might not have been there for all the notice that King took of him. Grimes was not put out; he ducked his head, winking at the others.

'Real high and mighty, ain't he? That's the way it oughter be. No nonsense about Mr King.'

King gave no indication that he had heard Grimes's words. He walked into the crescent of skulls and stared at the chair. The timber had come from the boat, washed up on the beach after the storm; it had been hacked to shape with the hatchet and the pieces had been lashed together with bark and creeper. The chair was ungainly but solid. King sat down and rested his hands on the arms.

'Is it okay, sir?' Fryer asked with mock obsequiousness. 'Is it to your liking?'

'It will serve,' King said. 'It is not good, but it will serve.'

The eyes under the peaked cap were no longer cold and dead; they shone as though a fever had been burning in them.

Meade came up behind Barlow. 'The throne of the King.' Meade's voice was sardonic. 'What decrees shall we have from the Seat of Judgement?'

King seemed to be in a trance. From where he sat it was possible to see a stretch of beach, and beyond the beach the startingly blue expanse of the ocean. Out there no moving thing was visible.

King roused himself. He began to

speak, slowly and with great deliberation.

'You are my people. You are my people for whom I am responsible. This chair is the symbol of that responsibility — and of my authority.'

He paused, gazed beyond them towards the sea, and went on: 'I have brought you out of the peril of great waters to the safety of this land. We are not a large community — thirteen souls in all — but the need for strict and impartial government is none the less for that. It is imperative that each and every one of you should act as an honourable and law-abiding citizen. There must be no indolence, no swinishness. Drunkenness will be punished severely; fornication also.'

Fryer said: 'How would we get drunk with no liquor?'

'There are ways of preparing strong drink,' King said. 'That will not be permitted.'

'And no love-making neither?' Fryer cast a sidelong glance at the three women. 'That's a bit hard, that is.'

'You heard what I said, Fryer. The laws

will be strictly enforced.'

Walsh broke in impatiently: 'What is all this nonsense? Really, King, why don't you do something about getting us away from here instead of indulging in all this ridiculous business of thrones and laws and God knows what? Have you gone out of your mind?'

Grimes looked round at Walsh and closed one eye. 'Now you're talking,' he whispered. 'If you ask me he's as batty as they come. But you got to humour him. He's got the revolver.'

King stared at Walsh for a while in silence before answering. Walsh became restive under the unwinking gaze of those fever-bright eyes. He shifted his bare feet with their dirty, untrimmed nails. Suppose Grimes were right. Certainly there was something very strange indeed about King.

King said at last: 'I am not out of my mind, Mr Walsh. It is necessary to make laws. Without them we sink into anarchy. Unbridled lusts become criminal acts and the result is death and destruction. Perhaps you do not realize the dangers of the pit on whose brink we stand. But I am able to see the fires burning.'

'What fires, Mr King?' Grimes asked softly.

'The fires of damnation,' King said.

Grimes looked round at Walsh and whispered: 'See what I mean? He's all the way round the bend and coming down the home straight. But you got to humour him.'

But Walsh was in no mood for humouring anyone. He wagged his forefinger at King and his voice became shrill and accusatory. 'You are a fool, sir. More than that, you are a criminal fool. It was your high-handed action that brought us to this pass. If any of us lose our lives, those lives will be on your head. I, sir, have a business in England. If, through my absence, that business fails I shall know where to lay the blame.'

'I care nothing for your petty business,' King said. He appeared unmoved by Walsh's tirade. 'I care nothing for your miserable money-grubbing. Perhaps I have done you a service in cutting you adrift from such follies. Here you may become a man. I do not guarantee that you will, but it is possible. We shall see.'

Walsh spluttered. 'Why, you — you madman.'

King said, and there was a bite in his voice: 'Have a care, Mr Walsh. I do not accept insults — from you or anyone.'

The revolver appeared suddenly in his hand as if he had conjured it out of the air. It was pointing at Walsh's stomach and not wavering. Walsh appeared to shrink; the striped pyjamas hung ridiculously on him and his lips quivered. There was no dignity about him, only fear.

Nobody moved; nobody said a word. Fryer and Grimes were grinning, enjoying Walsh's discomfiture. Meade had a worried expression on his face. Miss Partridge looked disapprovingly at the revolver; she pressed her thin lips together and shook her head reprovingly.

King said: 'You understand me, Mr Walsh?'

Walsh licked his lips and his voice shook. 'I understand. You don't need to point that gun at me. I understand perfectly.'

'Very well.'

King put the revolver back in his belt. He looked from one to another of the twelve men and women gathered in an arc in front of him, and a thin smile creased his face. It was such an unusual feature that there was something repellent about it; it was like a comic drawing on a gravestone; it was incongruous and vaguely horrifying. It made Helen Tudor feel sick.

'I think we can be very happy here,' King said. 'One big, happy family, is that not so? Just so long as you all remember to obey the law.'

9

Expedition

Barlow and Lanyon set off early in the morning. Barlow was eager to be away, for he felt that even now there was a possibility that King might take it into his unpredictable head to veto the expedition.

Katherine was depressed to see him go. 'I have a feeling that you may never come back.'

'I'll be back,' he said. 'Don't worry.'

'I wish you weren't going.'

'Somebody has got to go.'

They took with them the hatchet and their knives and a pocket compass. They took some dried fish and coconut, and water in flasks that they had salvaged from the boat. They were as well equipped as it was possible to be in the circumstances, but it was a meagre outfit with which to fit out an expedition.

They walked south along the beach

117

until they came to the stream and then followed the course of it inland. The trees and undergrowth became thicker as the ground rose, and the stream wound its way between rocks and boulders that were covered with luxuriant weeds and mosses. Here and there huge ferns sprouted in the hot, damp atmosphere.

It took them an hour to reach the pool into which the stream fell down a steep rock face. It seemed to have its origin in a spring gushing from a cleft in the rock some hundreds of feet higher up. As it dropped into the pool it made a constant rushing sound like that of wind passing through a forest. A curtain of spray hung where the falling water struck an outcrop, and this spray made a pleasant coolness in the air around the pool. Here the two men rested before starting on the long climb up the side of the mountain.

Barlow gazed upward and away to the left, assessing the prospect. 'There's the way,' he said, pointing.

The lower slopes were thickly covered with trees and other vegetation, but they knew that at the higher levels the trees thinned out, for it was possible to see the bare crest of the ridge from the beach.

'It'll be a hard climb,' Lanyon said. 'And what's on the other side?'

'When we can answer that question our job will be done.' Barlow stood up. 'Better be moving.'

Lanyon got to his feet also; then suddenly he seemed to stiffen, his head on one side as though listening.

'What is it, Wilf?' Barlow asked.

'I thought I heard something. Like a long wailing sound.'

'All I can hear is the waterfall.'

Lanyon relaxed slowly. 'It must have been imagination. Like seeing something that isn't there. And yet I could have sworn. Maybe there are ghost sounds.'

'Better not start thinking about ghosts,' Barlow said. 'Get started on that track and you'll end up as far round the bend as our friend King.'

'Not me,' Lanyon said. But Barlow noticed that there was an uneasy look in his eyes and that his hand was shaking. He began to wonder whether Lanyon was really the best kind of companion to have on a journey such as this. It might have been better to take Fryer or McKay.

They began to climb, moving away from the waterfall and searching out the easier slopes. It was hot and exhausting work, and the sweat poured from them, drenching their shirts. Soon the way became steeper and rockier, the trees giving way to scrub and bushes rooted in fissures.

'Who'd be a mountaineer?' Barlow said. 'Give me the sea any day.'

Lanyon made no answer. He was following some fifteen feet or so behind. Barlow looked back and thought that Lanyon's face looked pinched. He wondered whether the privations of the voyage had taken their toll of the engineer, leaving him in no state for the task in hand.

'Are you all right, Wilf? You're not sick?'

'I'm not sick,' Lanyon said, a little testily.

Barlow climbed on.

The sun was high now, a ball of fire in a brassy sky. They could no longer hear the sound of the waterfall or the surge of the ocean sweeping up the beach; all that had been left far behind. They paused to rest and Lanyon peered about him uneasily, distrust and fear in his eyes, as though he half expected an enemy to leap out from behind every rock.

'I don't like this place. There's something about it — I don't know what exactly — hard to explain. It's as if we were being watched. You think there's something behind you; you turn round and there's nothing. But it's still there; it's there all the time.'

'Steady now,' Barlow said. 'It's only the heat. Makes your head spin.'

Lanyon gave a nervous laugh. 'Yes, of course — the heat.' He scooped the sweat off his forehead with a finger, but Barlow noticed that soon he was glancing over his shoulder again.

'Come on,' Barlow said. 'We won't get anywhere like this. There's a long way to go.'

Lanyon did not move. 'Why go on?' he said. 'Where's the point? If we get to the top, what then?'

'Then we go down the other side.'

'And where does that take us?'

'I don't know.' Barlow was becoming impatient. 'Snap out of it, man. That's what we've come to find out.'

'It is?' Lanyon was sitting on his haunches, not looking at Barlow. 'Suppose we stop here for a time, then go back to the beach — tell them we couldn't find anything.'

'Hell of a lot of use that would be,' Barlow said. He stared at Lanyon. The engineer certainly looked ill. 'Look, if you're feeling bad maybe you'd better go back to the beach and I'll go on alone.'

Lanyon shook his head; it was obvious that the prospect of being left on his own did not appeal to him. 'No, Chris, I'm not as bad as that. I only thought that perhaps after all it was a waste of time. But if you mean to go on I'll come with you.'

'Let's be moving then.'

They began to climb again.

They had almost reached the summit when Barlow heard the sound. They were moving up a narrow gulley like a groove chiselled out of the side of the mountain. It was fairly steep, but with the help of their hands they were able to climb it with reasonable ease. In fact, for the whole of the way they had been able so to pick their route that nowhere had any real mountaineering skill been needed.

The sound appeared to be coming from above; it was a kind of low moaning, with sometimes a higher whistling note. And this time it was certainly not something that Lanyon had imagined.

Barlow stopped and listened; he looked down at Lanyon.

'You can hear it too?' Lanyon asked. He was obviously relieved when Barlow admitted that he could.

'No ghost this time, Wilf.'

'Then what is it?'

'That's what I intend to find out,' Barlow said.

He went on again with Lanyon following. The sound grew louder as they climbed. It was not continuous; sometimes it died away altogether, then it rose again, reached a peak, and once more faded away.

Lanyon said nervously: 'I think we ought to go back now.'

Barlow did not even pause. 'A sound can't hurt you.'

A few minutes later he had reached the crest and was standing on the ridge. On the landward side the mountain sloped down much more gently than on the side which they had just climbed. Soon it became lost in a dark green forest, so dense that from a distance it was impossible to distinguish separate trees. It was like gazing down on a broad, rolling canopy under which all life was hidden.

Lanyon came up and stood beside Barlow.

'There are the people who are making all the noise,' Barlow said, pointing. 'They won't hurt you.'

There were three of them, away to the left, the one in the middle taller than the other two. They appeared to have been fashioned out of the trunks of trees, and the middle one was perhaps fifteen feet high.

Lanyon stared at them. 'Idols. Carved Idols.'

They were not pretty objects; their very size made them grotesque, and the tops had been carved into the monstrous representation of human faces, with long, flattened noses and gaping mouths. The eyes were round black stones that reflected the light, so that they almost seemed to be alive. One could well imagine that those fantastic monsters were in fact watching.

'The Tate Gallery,' Barlow said.

They stood on a piece of flat ground in which they had been imbedded like three massive posts, but one of them had already begun to lean away from the other two. They were about thirty yards from where Barlow and Lanyon were standing, and they moaned and whistled like creatures suffering the torments of hell.

The two men crossed the intervening stretch of rocky ground and came to a halt in front of the idols, dwarfed by their gigantic size. Barlow tapped the wood with his knuckles; it had been bleached by sun and rain, and deep grooves had been eroded in its surface like the wrinkles in an old man's skin.

'Old,' Barlow said. 'Very, very old.'

Where the trunks entered the ground

there were signs of rotting. It would not be many more years before all three had fallen to the dust in which they would gradually moulder away. They were gods, but they were mortal, even as the men who had created them.

'Ingenious bits of work,' Barlow said. 'You see how the sound is produced?'

He pointed to the trunk of the middle idol. There was a vertical slit in it, and inside the wood had been hollowed out, forming a primitive kind of organ pipe. Wind blowing into the slit made the sounds which came out of the idol's mouth.

'Enough to give anyone the shivers,' Lanyon said.

'Possibly what they were meant to do. To scare away evil spirits perhaps.'

'Who do you think put them there?'

'Your guess is as good as mine. The owners of those skulls maybe. Or, more likely, the people who captured those skulls.'

Lanyon looked down towards the distant green of the jungle stretching away below — secret, mysterious, seemingly limitless; like a trap waiting for them to step inside.

'Where do we go from here?'

'Down there,' Barlow said.

Again the expression of uneasiness, even of fear, came into Lanyon's eyes. He said hesitantly: 'What do you expect to find?'

Barlow answered impatiently: 'I don't have any expectations. I just mean to go and look. That's what we came to do, isn't it?'

'I suppose so,' Lanyon admitted. But he showed no eagerness to start moving. With each succeeding step that they had taken he had become apparently less and less inclined to go farther. Barlow could not understand it; Lanyon had seemed willing enough to come with him at first; but since the moment when they had rested by the waterfall it was as though some strange fear had got into him, some terror of this unknown country that made him reluctant to go on.

But there was a job to be done, and Lanyon, whatever his misgivings, had got to be pricked into action.

Barlow said roughly: 'You bet so. Let's be on our way. We've wasted enough time with these characters.'

He set off quickly down the eastern slope and did not look back. After a few moments he could hear Lanyon behind him, hurrying to catch up. The engineer might be afraid of the jungle, but it was evident that he was even more afraid of being left alone. He wanted Barlow's company.

When Barlow did at last glance back the three idols had disappeared from sight and the moaning of the wind in their hollow stomachs had faded too.

Barlow and Lanyon went down into the green and humid chambers of the forest.

At nightfall the jungle seemed to burst into life with the explosiveness of a bomb. It shouted and gibbered and wailed. There were loud rustling noises, the sound of furtive movements, the ticking and buzzing of myriads of insects, the croaking of frogs and the leathery beating of the wings of giant bats.

The two men made a rough platform of branches on which to sleep. They pulled the leeches from their legs, ate a frugal meal and lay down. Barlow could feel Lanyon shivering, whether from cold, fever or terror he could not tell.

He said: 'Can't you sleep, Wilf?'

'Sleep!' Lanyon seemed to consider the question utterly ridiculous. 'Who could sleep here?'

'Better try. We've got a long day ahead of us tomorrow.'

He could not see Lanyon. The darkness was thick and muddy and impenetrable; it was like a heavy curtain enveloping them.

'Tomorrow we'll head east again. We may come to a river. There's bound to be a settlement, a village somewhere. We'll just have to keep pressing on. That's all there is to it.'

Lanyon did not answer.

'Gone to sleep,' Barlow muttered. 'Well, good luck to him. Better get some myself.'

Lanyon lay on his back, staring up into the darkness and trying to contain his terror, trying not to scream. And all the noises of the jungle night beat upon the quivering defences of his mind.

★ ★ ★

They started as soon as it was light in the morning. Barlow was concerned about Lanyon; he thought the engineer looked sicker than ever. There were dark patches under Lanyon's eyes and his face was haggard.

'How did you sleep?' Barlow asked.

'I didn't,' Lanyon said. 'Did you?'

'A little. It wasn't the best of hotels. Maybe we'll find a village tonight.'

But it was to be five days before they were to find anything of that description, and then it was to be not what they had hoped for.

They continued to travel east, away from the coast, guided by the pocket compass that Barlow was carrying. It was hard going through difficult country. In some places it was necessary to cut a way through with the hatchet; in other places the jungle thinned out and there were patches of relatively open ground. They saw brightly coloured parrots and butter-flies, and were plagued by flies and leeches.

130

They had been travelling for two days when the water barred their way. It was not a great river but it was far too wide and deep for them to hope of crossing it even if they had wished to do so. It looked brown and muddy; here and there were eddies and ripples that gave evidence of a rapid current. Trees grew close to the bank on both sides and dipped their hanging branches in the stream; roots stood out, festooned with slime and dripping weed; there was a pervading odour of fungus and decay.

Barlow's own reflection stared up at him from the water; it looked wild and unkempt, and it came as something of a shock to realize that this bearded face with the shaggy, uncombed hair above it was indeed his. He wondered how long it took for a man to slough off all the manners and restraints of civilization as he had sloughed the shaven face and the trimmed hair; how long before men who had come to look like beasts became beasts in fact.

He stood up and stared at Lanyon. Perhaps it was something strange and animal in his eyes that made Lanyon instinctively draw back a pace.

'What's wrong, Wilf?' Barlow asked.

'How do you mean?' Lanyon was looking at him warily.

'Have you seen a ghost?'

Lanyon shook his head. 'Only you.'

Barlow turned away from him and gazed at the river. 'If only we had a canoe this could help. As it is, we shall just have to push on by the same means as before. Upstream or down?'

'Whichever you say.'

'Don't you have any ideas?'

'I leave it to you.' There was a weary, hopeless note in Lanyon's voice. He looked exhausted; Barlow wondered whether he had slept at all since leaving the beach. He was beginning to be afraid for Lanyon, afraid that the young engineer was cracking.

He made a decision. 'We'll go downstream.'

★ ★ ★

It was three days later when they came to the village. There were a few rough huts

132

standing up on stilts, but no sign of people. The silence was broken only by the screeching of birds.

'I don't like it,' Lanyon said. He had come to a halt.

'What are you stopping for?' Barlow asked. 'Let's go and investigate.'

'Not me.'

With a curse Barlow left him and walked to the first hut. It had a raised floor with rough steps leading up to it. Barlow went up the steps and peered into the hut. It was shadowy inside and at first he could see nothing; then, as his eyes became accustomed to the gloom, he made out something pale lying on the floor. Closer investigation proved what he had already guessed: it was a human skeleton. It was not alone; there were four in the hut; two of them had been children.

Barlow went to the other huts and peered into them all. He found other skeletons, no one living. They had all been dead a long time and the huts were rotting.

He went back to where Lanyon was waiting.

'What did you find?' Lanyon asked.

'Nothing but bones. It looks to me as though some pestilence struck the village. Either that or they were attacked by some hostile tribe, but I don't think that's likely.'

'Why not?'

'They've all got their heads.' Barlow said. 'Are you ready?'

Lanyon looked startled. 'Ready for what?'

'To go on. There's no help for us here.'

Lanyon did not move. 'I think we ought to go back,' he said. 'We're not getting anywhere.'

'You can go back,' Barlow said. 'I'm going on.'

He turned and walked away. When he looked back he saw that Lanyon was following.

10

Flight Into Darkness

When Barlow awoke in the darkness he sensed at once that something was wrong. He listened and could hear no sound from Lanyon. He put out his hand and could not find his companion; Lanyon was not there.

Barlow crawled out from the rough shelter of leaves and branches and found that the moon was shining. He looked across the area of open ground at the edge of which they had built the shelter, and it was washed with moonlight. Nothing was moving in that enclosure fenced in by the walls of the jungle. From the forest came the cacophony of the night-watchers, the creatures that moved in darkness, the hunters and the hunted.

Barlow shouted: 'Wilf! Hi, there! Where are you?'

There was no answer to his call. And

then he saw a shadow moving; but it was not a shadow, it was a man, bent almost double, running across the patch of moonlight. It was Lanyon.

Barlow ran after him, shouting to him to stop, to come back. He saw Lanyon glance over his shoulder; the moonlight caught his face for a moment; but he did not halt in his running, rather did he seem to increase his pace, as though in that backward glance he had caught a glimpse of that which he believed to be pursuing him, that from which he must at all cost make his escape.

He reached the edge of the clearing and disappeared among the trees. He was still bent low, so that in running he looked more like a wild animal than a man.

Barlow followed across the open ground, moving rapidly. When he came to the far side he paused and listened. In front of him the thickness of the jungle was penetrated only here and there by stray shafts of moonlight, and to keep in touch with Lanyon in there would have been an impossible task.

He shouted again: 'Where are you, Wilf?

It's me — Chris. Come back, you damned fool.'

He heard a sudden movement surprisingly close to him, and then the rustling of foliage. It might have been Lanyon; he might have been waiting, hidden in the undergrowth. If so, Barlow's shout had served only to frighten him again, and he had rushed away into the darkness.

But the sound gave Barlow a lead and he followed it. Something rope-like coiled itself about his ankle and he fell heavily, jarring his ribs. He got up at once and continued to follow the sound of Lanyon's retreat. He could hear him now uttering little cries and yelps of terror.

Barlow realized that he would have to catch the engineer or the man would be lost for ever. Lanyon's fears had finally become too strong for him to bear, and now he was running away from something which there was no hope of outstripping because it had its origin in the dark recesses of his own tormented mind.

Barlow pressed on. If he could only catch up with Lanyon he might be able to reason with him. If he could only hold him until daylight came to relieve his fears, then they could abandon the expedition and start back towards the beach, for it was certain now that they could go no farther. Once back with the others, Lanyon might recover; but it was certain that in the jungle he was lost, a man wandering in the grip of an unending nightmare.

Then he heard Lanyon scream. The scream seemed to vibrate on the senses, and it was followed by another and another.

Barlow ran forward and came suddenly to an opening in the forest where the moonlight penetrated through the roof of foliage. It shone on Lanyon, on his head and shoulders; there was no more of him than that still above ground. He was in a pit of slime and still sinking.

Barlow drew back just in time; his own feet had begun to sink into the morass.

Lanyon had stopped screaming; he was making small whimpering noises and scrabbling ineffectually at the slime with his hands.

Barlow shouted to him: 'Spread your

arms wide and don't struggle.' But Lanyon only stared back at him with horror and continued to move his arms in a jerky, convulsive manner that merely stirred the morass, releasing nauseating odours and smearing the mud over his face and hair.

Barlow broke a small branch from a tree and pushed one end towards Lanyon, shouting to him. 'Grab it, Wilf. Grab it, can't you?'

But Lanyon made no attempt to grasp the branch. In fact it seemed that he was not only struggling to free himself from the grip of the morass but at the same time was trying desperately to get away from Barlow. It was as though in Barlow he saw, not a friend, but the personification of that very horror from which he had been fleeing. Perhaps in his crazed mind the clinging mud and the figure leaning towards him with the branch were both part of the same fearsome spectre that had driven him to seek refuge in the hidden places of the jungle.

'For God's sake, grab it, Wilf,' Barlow cried. 'It's your only chance. Grab it and

I'll pull you out.'

Lanyon threw up his hands in front of his face as though to shield his eyes from some awful sight. The hands were dripping with black slime. He had begun to scream again.

Barlow took one pace forward and felt his foot sink in up to the ankle. He pulled back and the foot came out slowly with a glutinous sucking noise. Bubbles of gas came up and burst on the surface, emitting a stench of corruption.

Suddenly Lanyon stopped screaming. The mud had gagged him; it went into his mouth and clogged his throat. It rose higher; it reached his nostrils.

Barlow watched helplessly. There was nothing he could do now. The moonlight slanted down and caught Lanyon's eyes; they seemed to glitter for a moment and then they were blotted out. The last that Barlow saw of the engineer was one finger moving spasmodically just above the surface of the morass; then it too had gone and there was nothing to be seen but the stirred-up mud shining blackly under the cold light of the moon.

★　★　★

Barlow came again to the village on his
way back. Oppressed by the brooding
silence of death, he passed through
hurriedly. He had a sensation of being
watched; it was as though the dead men,
the skeletons, were spying on him from
the shadow of the huts; as though, when
he had passed by, they came out and
followed him. So powerful did this
impression become that he was unable to
resist the urge to swing round in an
attempt to catch them at it.

There was no one; only the silent,
decaying huts and the encroaching jungle.

'This won't do,' Barlow muttered. 'This
was the way Lanyon went. Mustn't get
like him. Got to keep a grip — got to.'

He pressed on through the village. He
was going back to the beach, his mission a
failure. Perhaps he ought to have gone on,
but now that Lanyon was dead he
experienced a terrible feeling of loneli-
ness; he felt that what he wanted above all
else was to see another living human
being, to hear a friendly voice. He craved

the society of his own people to drive away the ghosts that were haunting his mind. The jungle had closed in upon him and he felt oppressed by it. He had to get back.

★ ★ ★

He could not tell how long the nightmare lasted, whether days or weeks or months. He lost the river; he lost the hatchet and the compass; he stumbled on without direction, caught in the limitless, entwining tendrils of the jungle. He filled his ravenous stomach with strange and loathsome foods, with grubs found under the bark of rotting logs, with roots and berries. He drank from stagnant pools of muddy water and from hollows in the boles of trees. One day he killed a small snake with a stick. He skinned it with his knife and ate it raw, scarcely aware of the taste. On some days it rained endlessly; every leaf and branch dripped water and he was drenched to the skin.

He was haunted always by a fear of that madness which had taken Lanyon and might claim him also. He thought that perhaps he was going round in circles and always coming back to the same spot. And indeed it seemed that this was so, for one day he stumbled once again on the dead village, and pushing his way into one of the huts, he saw the skeletons still lying there as before.

He tried to take a grip on himself. He had to find the river and follow it upstream to the point where he and Lanyon had joined it. He had been a fool to lose the compass, but the hatchet was perhaps an even more serious loss; he had no idea where he had left it and could not remember when he had last had it in his hand.

Taking his direction from the village, he found the river at last, and he went back upstream for four days without being able to discover the place where he had first come upon it. Everywhere looked the same; there was nothing to distinguish one part of the bank from another.

He felt now that his strength was failing. At night he found it difficult to sleep. He was tormented by flies and

143

leeches, surrounded by the weird screaming and chattering of the jungle, and
utterly alone. When he did sleep he was
plagued by nightmares. He dreamed that
he was being pursued by Lanyon, the mud
of the pit constantly dripping from his
jaws and nostrils and the tips of his
outstretched fingers. He awoke sweating
and shivering.

* * *

He left the river at last and bore away
westward, gauging his direction by those
glimpses of the sun that he was able to
catch through the canopy of trees. But he
could find nothing that was recognisable
from his outward journey, no landmark to
tell him that he was indeed travelling in
the right direction.

One day he came upon a pool of water
that was clear enough to serve as a mirror.
He was down on his hands and knees
ready to lap it up like a dog when he saw
the wild eyes staring up at him from a
tangle of hair.

'Can this be me?' he muttered. 'This

animal. Is this Christopher Barlow, once bosun of the *Southern Pioneer*? When was that? How many centuries ago? In what past existence?'

In a fit of rage and despair he broke the image with his fist. He plunged his face into the pool and drank. And the water tasted sour and stagnant, biting at his throat.

It was after midday when he came to the mountain. He stepped out of the jungle and saw it climbing away ahead of him, trees and bushes scattered about its landward slopes. He had been exhausted, but the sight of the mountain invigorated him. He had almost lost hope, but now hope returned in a flood; it was like an elixir of life poured into a worn-out body.

'It is there,' he cried. 'It is; it is.'

He began the ascent at once, feverishly eager to reach the summit. He had under-estimated the distance and over-estimated his own strength. Many times he was forced to sit down and rest before he was able to go on. It was evening when at last he stood upon the ridge and saw the three idols.

He ran towards them with a drunken, staggering run, and heard again the moaning and whistling of the wind in their hollow bellies. He put his arms about the middle idol and kissed the weathered timber of its trunk. The three idols stared straight ahead, heedless of the weakness of the man. For a long time Barlow lay at their feet, letting the strength flow back into his limbs.

11

Return to the Beach

It had begun to grow dark when Barlow roused himself. He was eager now to descend the shoreward side of the mountain. He wanted to see the faces of the others; especially he wanted to see Katherine. And now that he was so close again to the beach he began to have fears that they might not be there.

He had been so long in the jungle; how many days, how many weeks, he could not tell. Suppose that, during that time, a ship had come and rescued the others; or suppose they too, tired of waiting for the return of Lanyon and himself, had set off on a journey to the interior. Suppose he should find the beach deserted, the caves abandoned, the chair of authority that King had had constructed no longer occupied. These thoughts plagued his mind as he set off recklessly down the slope. He had to get back without delay and see for himself.

He had forgotten how much steeper this side of the mountain was than the landward side, and in his impetuosity he almost sent himself plunging headlong down to the bottom. A bush that he was able to grasp saved him, and from that point onward he took greater care, moving more slowly and testing the ground below him for any treacherous looseness.

Darkness fell like a cloak, but now Barlow could hear the sound of the waterfall away to his right, and the sound drew him, an utterly weary man groping his way between rocks and bushes. In this manner he had descended more than half the distance when, probing with his left foot in a cautious search for a hold, he suddenly found nothing beneath him but empty air.

The left leg dangled in space and he hung there, clinging on with his fingers and scrabbling with his right foot in a desperate search for some ledge or fissure with the help of which he might hoist himself up from this precipice on which he had stumbled in the darkness. He could not tell how great a drop lay below him; it might be only a few feet; it might equally well be a hundred. All he could see when he glanced down was a black pit.

His right foot slipped a few inches and some loose stones went over the ledge; he listened for the sound of their dropping but could hear only the waterfall. He felt his finger-nails tearing.

He was sweating as he lay there in the darkness with one leg dangling and the other doubled up beneath him. He tried again to drag himself up, but the right foot began to slip again as he moved, and his whole body slid a little nearer to the edge. He froze into immobility, hanging like a limpet to the rock, unable to move upward and terrified of slipping down.

Sweat streamed down the back of his neck and trickled between his shoulder-blades. His right foot slipped again; he tried to find a grip for it, but it slipped further; it went over the ledge into space with the left one. First one hand lost its hold, then the other. His nails broke and his fingers could not hold him. He went over the edge and began to fall.

★ ★ ★

The moon was shining when Barlow opened his eyes. He was lying on his back under the shadow of an outcrop of rock. He looked up and could see, no more than twenty feet above him, the ledge from which he had fallen. The sheer face was in fact no more than ten feet in height and gave way lower down to a slope which ended at the rock under which Barlow was lying and on which he had undoubtedly struck his head when he fell.

The head throbbed violently. His probing fingers discovered a gash under the matted hair, sticky with half-congealed blood.

He wondered how long he had been unconscious. The fact that the moon had now risen proved that he had been lying there an appreciable length of time. He struggled to a sitting position, and the head was like a gong booming. He felt sick and his bones ached as though he had been beaten with a club.

But his mind was clear. Perhaps the blow had knocked out that lingering hint of madness. He knew now what he would do: he would go to the pool below the waterfall, he would bathe himself, cleaning off the filth of the jungle, and then he would go to the beach. If the others had left, there would surely be some message for him. They would not have gone away without leaving for him and Lanyon a clue to where they had gone.

He got to his feet, tested each of his limbs in turn to make sure that no bones were broken, and then continued on his way down the mountain.

When he came to the pool he stripped to the skin and stepped into the water. He felt the shock of it like a current of electricity galvanizing his body. He began to wash the mud from his skin; he dipped his head beneath the surface and felt the sharp bite of the water as it probed his wound.

He stepped out of the pool with the silver drops of water glittering on his body. He shook himself and rubbed the skin with his hands, massaging warmth back into his limbs. When he was reasonably dry he donned once more his ragged and filthy clothes, doing so with some reluctance and distaste. He had thought of washing them also, but had decided against it, since there would have been no way of drying them quickly.

He fastened about his waist the belt of plaited leather from which hung his knife in its pigskin sheath, then set off towards the shore.

★ ★ ★

The beach was like silver, and beyond it the sea moved gently, coming in with a hiss as it rolled over on to the sand, advancing and retreating and advancing again like an army unwilling, though constantly repulsed, to give up the attack.

Barlow came out from the shadow of the palm trees and walked down to the edge of the water. He stood there for a time with the small waves lapping at his feet, staring out across the burnished surface of the sea, along the gleaming pathway of the moon.

When he turned he saw the girl. She was motionless, watching him, her hands hanging by her sides. A breath of wind ruffled her hair and blew her skirt out on one side; then the wind dropped and the skirt fell back into place.

She moved towards him, slowly at first, as though unsure of herself and of him also. Then, as doubt vanished, she began to run, her bare feet kicking up little spurts of sand and her hair flying. Then when she had come within a yard or two of him she stopped again.

'Chris,' she said. 'It is you. Oh, thank God.'

When he looked at her closely he could see the tears glittering in her eyes and beginning to roll down her cheeks.

'It's all right, Katie. It's all right.'

'I thought you were never coming back. I was afraid you might be dead.'

'Not me.'

'You've been away so long.'

'How long?'

'Don't you know?'

'No,' he said. 'I lost count.'

'Three weeks. More.'

'As long as that?' And yet it could have been so much longer. It had seemed like a lifetime.

'I've missed you, Chris. I've missed you terribly. If you hadn't come back — '

'But I have come back,' he said. 'And I've missed you too.'

Yet, even as he said it, he knew that this was not entirely true. He had scarcely thought of her; there had been too many other things on his mind.

Suddenly, as though the thought had only just come to her, she said: 'Where's Wilfred?'

'He's dead,' Barlow said.

She looked horrified. 'Oh, no. Not dead.'

'Yes.'

'But how did he die?'

'He fell into a morass. I tried to pull him out. It wasn't possible.' He felt a sudden wave of anger at the memory of Lanyon's death. He added harshly: 'You can't pull a man out of hell.'

Some time later she asked: 'Did you find anything?'

'A village. That was dead too.'

'Dead?' She did not understand.

'Nothing but skeletons. Maybe some epidemic hit them. No help there.'

He began to walk with her along the beach, heading for the caves.

'Why are you out anyway?' he asked. 'Why aren't you asleep?'

'I couldn't sleep. I felt I had to get out of the cave. Perhaps something told me you would come back tonight.'

'What's happened since I've been away?'

'Nothing good. I've been afraid.'

'Is Mr King worse?'

'Yes. And he's driven Copley away.'

'Driven him away? Where?'

'Anywhere. Out of the caves. Off the beach. Mr King has given orders that he is not to be allowed back. He says that if he sees Copley he'll shoot him. And I believe he will.'

'What did Copley do?'

'He broke the law. He went into the women's cave. King sat on his throne and passed judgement on him; it would have been laughable if it hadn't been so serious.

He sentenced Copley to banishment.'

'But surely the others wouldn't stand for that. They wouldn't let him get away with it.'

'They didn't help Copley. They seemed to think it was a joke. Fryer even helped to drive Copley away with the boat-hook. Mr Walsh protested a bit, but nobody paid any attention to him. Miss Partridge protested more strongly, but Mr King told her to hold her tongue.'

'How long ago was this?'

'Oh soon after you left.'

'And Copley hasn't been back?'

'Nobody has seen him. Perhaps he's dead.'

Barlow slapped his hand against his thigh. 'That madman King is going too far. He's got to be stopped.'

'He has the revolver,' Katherine said.

12

Dangerous Situation

King sat on the chair within the semi-circle of skulls with his peaked cap on his head and the sun shining on him. His beard was speckled with grey hairs and his eyes were fever-bright. He was thinner than he had been when Barlow had seen him last; in fact he had a skeleton look about him that matched the surrounding skulls; it was as though all traces of flesh were being burnt away by the fire within him to leave only a parchment skin stretched over the bones. His voice sounded more metallic than ever.

'So Mr Lanyon is dead?'

'That's right, sir,' Barlow said.

King nodded with great deliberation and Barlow could almost imagine that he heard the scraggy neck creaking. The neck was all cords and hollows with the Adam's apple as prominent as a door-knob. When King swallowed it jumped up and down in a kind of nervous dance. Everything about King was somehow bizarre; it might have been amusing to watch his antics if he had not had the power of life and death. The power was there for all to see, thrust into his belt, the butt protruding.

'Copley has gone from us also,' King said. 'I have banished him. Our numbers are thus reduced to eleven.' His head did not move but his gaze shifted from one to another of the men and women who were gathered in front of him. 'We were orginally thirteen, and there are some who might consider that an unlucky number. That is superstition. There is no luck in numbers, good or bad.'

Fryer laughed. 'Thirteen was bad luck for Copley; it was bad luck for Mr Lanyon. Maybe it'll be bad luck for the flaming lot of us.'

King said coldly: 'You are a fool, Fryer. A bag of wind. You will oblige me by not thrusting your opinions upon us.'

Fryer seemed to be in half a mind to attack King, but he looked at the revolver and decided against any such action. He gave another laugh, though he did not seem amused.

'You're a funny man, Mr King. You say some funny things, damn me if you don't.' He turned away and Barlow heard him add in a much lower tone: 'Maybe some day it don't sound so bleeding funny. No, sir.'

The tension that had built up for the moment evaporated.

Walsh said: 'All the same, King, thirteen or not, you have to admit we've been pretty unfortunate since we left the *Southern Pioneer*.'

Three weeks had not improved Walsh's appearance. He looked dirty and haggard, and there was a nervous tic in his left cheek that he could not control; it affected his left eye also, so that he seemed to be continually winking. His pyjamas being scarcely decent, he wore the dressing-gown for most of the time; in it he had something of the look of a run-down patrician of ancient Rome, a senator fallen on hard times.

King looked at him with undisguised

contempt. 'I do not agree. We are as well off now as we have ever been. We have food, we have shelter. What have we lost but the feverish chasing after money that is the curse of civilization. Here we may live in contentment, needing nothing.'

It was Grimes who said in his sly manner, seeming to drop the words out of the corner of his mouth: 'We could do with some beer and fags.'

'You are better without alcohol or tobacco,' King said. 'They are both poisons.'

'Gimme the poison then,' Grimes muttered.

King dismissed the assembly with a final gesture of his hand, as a monarch might dismiss his subjects. The group split up, but Meade laid a hand on Barlow's arm and drew him aside. He made a sign to Walsh and the older man joined them.

'What did you find?' Meade asked.

'I've told you,' Barlow said. 'I found the jungle and a river and a dead village. Nothing to help us.'

Meade said thoughtfully: 'Then if we don't help ourselves we've had it. That's the long and the short of it.'

'How do you mean?'

Meade shrugged. 'You've seen King. He's as mad as a hatter and getting worse. He's playing God and enjoying it. Copley was only the first; there'll be others. I tell you we're sitting on a time-bomb. Soon there'll be one hell of an explosion if we don't get away from here or do something else about it.'

'I agree,' Walsh said. 'It is a dangerous situation. There's going to be bad trouble before long.'

Barlow could see that the other two were scared. In a tight corner he did not believe that either of them would prove to be much more use than Lanyon.

'What do you suggest?'

Meade was silent. Walsh said: 'Wouldn't it be possible to make a boat?'

'Are you a carpenter?'

Walsh shook his head. 'I thought you might be able to do something in that line. You're a seaman.'

'Do you realize, Mr Walsh, what kind of a boat would be needed? It's not just a question of making something that will float. It would have to be the kind you could navigate.'

'You think it couldn't be done then?'

'Even if it could, I don't think King would permit it. It looks as though he's made up his mind to stay here, to establish his kingdom.'

Meade snorted. 'That skinny, crack-brained old bastard. We can get rid of him.'

'In what way?'

Meade drew a finger across his throat. 'The easiest way. No return ticket.'

'No,' Barlow said.

'It's our lives or his. What do you say, Walsh?'

Walsh looked uneasy. 'I don't know. I don't know at all. I don't like the sound of it.'

'He's mad, isn't he? It would be the kindest way.'

'I don't agree with killing. I don't like it.'

'Ah, you're too soft. In a situation like this you have to forget about the niceties of civilization. You can't afford to be squeamish. Am I right, bosun?'

'No,' Barlow said again.

'Oh, to hell with it then,' Meade said. He turned away and went striding off along the beach, hands in pockets, shoulders hunched. Barlow saw Helen Tudor run to join him. The two of them walked away together.

'That woman's in love with Meade,' Walsh said. 'There's no future in it, the way we're fixed.'

'There never would have been any future in it,' Barlow said.

* * *

Meade walked along the beach with Helen Tudor, trying to think of a way of getting rid of King. It seemed to him that it was King alone who stood in the way of an escape from this captivity. For it was captivity. It might be all right for a man who liked the simple life, a hermit content with the basic necessities; but it was not for him; he wanted something more; he wanted amusement, the bright lights of the cities of the world, theatres, night-clubs, the lot. And here he was stuck on

163

this damned strip of beach while a crazy sailor with a revolver proclaimed his own brand of law and order and made no attempt whatever to get away.

Helen Tudor looked at his set face and the folds of anger in his forehead. She pressed his arm.

'What are you thinking about?'

'About a man who's made himself king in fact as well as name. God too maybe.'

'Why think about him, Arnold? Why not make the best of things as they are?'

'The best of things!' He stared at her in amazement. 'How the devil can you make the best of things? We're wasting time here. Don't you see? We're wasting time we can never get back. My career is being ruined.'

For the moment he had forgotten that his career was no longer on the up-grade, that he had gone over the top and was on the way down. In his resentment he had convinced himself that only this disaster stood between him and the really big money.

'I'm rusting here. I ought to have a racket in my hand. It'll take months to get back into form — months. I can't afford the time.'

'Yes, I can see that. It's hard on you. You've had a tough break.'

'It's hard on you too, isn't it?' Meade said grudgingly. 'You're marking time here. You're not getting those fat contracts.'

She made a grimace. 'What fat contracts would they be? Might as well face the truth — I never was much good. Oh, I know I made out I was great, but I wasn't and never could be. There comes a time when you might as well admit the facts. I haven't lost so much.'

What had she lost but dirty theatres and tenth-rate nightclubs, half-hearted applause and seedy dressing-rooms? And in exchange she had gained Arnold Meade. Here he was hers and there was no one to take him away from her. Here she knew that he would not drift out of town and leave her with nothing but a memory.

But if they should ever get back to civilization she knew that she would lose him. There would be other attractions, other women; and he would leave her perhaps without even saying good-bye. She had no illusions about Meade; she knew that he was selfish and had no strength of character, that he was inferior to Chris Barlow, even in a way to Stephen Walsh; she knew that he was no good to her, that he did not really love her and only pretended to do so because she was there and it was the easiest way; but all this made no difference. She was in love with him and for her there was no way out. That was why she no longer looked upon this stretch of coast as a prison; she loved it because he was there also.

Meade said, harping on the grudge: 'It's King who's to blame. I believe he had all this figured out from the start. Maybe he was responsible for blowing up the ship.'

'Oh, no, he couldn't have done that.'

'I wouldn't put it beyond him. I believe he wanted to get us all here so that he could play God. That's his special mania.'

'What are you going to do?'

'What can I do?' He picked up a pebble and flung it petulantly into the sea. 'There just isn't a damn thing I can do. That's the hell of it.' He paused, then added softly: 'Unless I kill King.'

She gripped his arm. 'No. You mustn't even think of that. But I know you'd never do it. Not you, Arnold.'

He almost hated her then because he knew that she was right. He knew that he would never have the guts to do it. To do a thing like that you had to have something that just was not in his make-up. But somebody else might do it.

'And even if you did kill King,' Helen said, 'it wouldn't help. You still wouldn't be able to get away.'

★　★　★

It was the cry that woke Barlow. He lay in the darkness and waited for it to be repeated. He could see the entrance to the cave as a pale area of light and around him he could hear the heavy breathing of the sleeping men.

A minute passed and he wondered whether he had been mistaken, whether the cry had merely been a part of some dream from which he had awakened. But then the cry came again, and it was nearer this time. It sounded half-human and half-animal.

He got up from the bed of leaves and dried seaweed on which he had been lying and crouched in the darkness. No one else was stirring; apparently he was the only one who had been roused by the cry. Stepping carefully to avoid the others, he moved to the entrance and went outside.

It was moonlight and there was no cloud. Away on his right he could hear the hiss of the sea as it rolled up the beach. He halted in the entrance under the overhang of the cliff and waited for the cry to come again. He waited for several minutes, motionless, staring at the patches of moonlight and the dark trees, watching for the creature, either animal or human, to come out into the open.

Then he saw it, and at once he stiffened, his scalp pricking. It came stealthily out from the cover of the trees and slunk into the moonlight. It was naked and it was a man, but bent so low that it might almost have been running on all fours, the shaggy, unkempt head thrust forward questingly.

It did not cry out again, not loudly, but a low whimpering sound broke from it, such as a dog might make when trying to get into a house from which it had been shut out. The head moved constantly from side to side, watchful and wary.

Barlow called softly: 'Copley! Arthur Copley!'

The thing lifted its head slightly but made no other sign of having heard. It began to move across the moonlit space towards the cliff and the caves. He stepped forward to meet it, but before he had taken more than four paces he saw a red dagger of flame stabbing the shadows and heard the crack of the revolver.

Without a sound the creature, the outcast, rolled over and lay stretched out on the ground. When Barlow reached it the limbs were still twitching.

He kneeled down and saw the dark hole in the chest; he saw too the bones almost poking through the skin; he saw the festering sores, the scars, the filth. It was Copley sure enough, Copley with his hare-lip and his black hair, Copley who had been banished from King's little kingdom and had had the temerity to return.

Barlow heard a movement. He looked up and saw King silhouetted against the sky with the revolver still in his hand.

'You killed him,' Barlow said in a hard, bitter voice. 'You damned bloody murderer. You killed him.'

King answered without emotion: 'He had been warned. I told him I would shoot him if he dared to come back. He chose to ignore my orders.'

He thrust the revolver back in his belt, turned and walked away. For him the incident was finished.

13

Jetsam

It rained all morning. They stayed in the caves, listening to the dripping of the rain and hating one another with a hatred born of enforced idleness.

Without any discussion on the subject the men had split into two groups: on the one side were Fryer, Grimes, Lynch and McKay, and on the other were Meade, Walsh and Barlow. King belonged to neither group; he was the head of them all, isolated in the exercise of his authority, allying himself neither to one side nor the other, above such petty tensions.

The women were on the side of Meade and Walsh and Barlow; it was a natural loyalty, and it was something that injected an extra bitterness into the rivalry.

The rain fell steadily, without pause, and the air was warm and humid. The walls of the cave where the men crouched ran with moisture.

'Nice day for ducks,' Grimes said. 'If there was any ducks. How long we gotta put up with this?'

'It could rain for days,' Lynch said. 'Maybe weeks, once it starts. No telling.'

'That'd be nice, that would. Cooped up here with nothing to do but twiddle our thumbs.'

'And no fags,' Lynch grumbled. 'Here's me gasping for a spit and a draw. We got none of the comforts of life.'

Fryer was tracing lines on the floor of the cave with the point of his sheath-knife. It was so gloomy that he could hardly see what he had drawn. He looked up slyly, tapping the knife-blade on the palm of his hand.

'There's some do all right for a certain class of comfort. Take Mr Meade and the bosun here. They got their fancy women. Maybe Mr Walsh too, I shouldn't wonder.'

'Stow it,' Barlow said.

Fryer refused to stow it. 'It oughta be share and share alike. We're all in the same boat, or maybe I should say out of the same boat, so there oughtn't to be no

172

favouritism. What's right for one is right for another, that's how I look at it.'

Barlow moved towards Fryer in the damp gloom of the cave. Walsh peered nervously from the shadows, hoping there would be no violence. He did not like violence; it made him physically sick. Meade watched also, but with less concern; it was something to relieve the monotony, and they could certainly do with some relief.

'I said stow it, Ben.' There was an edge to Barlow's voice.

Fryer held the knife loosely in his right hand; it might have been there by accident; he might not have been aware of it. But all the others knew that it was there and nobody was saying anything; they were just watching.

'I can say what I like, when I like and where I like. No bloody bosun tells me what to say and what not to say. What's so sacred about them women in the other cave? They're females, ain't they?'

'I'm warning you, Ben,' Barlow said. He watched Fryer, watched the knife. He was remembering that Fryer had helped to drive poor Copley away with the boat-hook. It was just one more item on the slate. 'I'm warning you.'

'That for your warning,' Fryer said, and he spat in Barlow's face.

Barlow's hands moved so fast that Walsh could not follow them. He saw the glitter of the knife as it flew out of Fryer's hand; he heard the ring of the steel as it fell to the ground. Then he saw Fryer's head jerk back and strike the solid rock of the cave wall. Fryer slumped down and lay motionless where he had fallen.

Barlow picked up the knife, balanced it in his hand for a moment and then tossed it away.

'It's stopped raining,' he said. 'We can go out now and get some fresh air. Maybe we need it.'

Walsh came out of the shadows and looked down at Fryer. Fryer was breathing noisily but he was still not moving.

'Will he be all right? You didn't injure him, I hope.'

Barlow laughed. 'With a head like that? You'd need a sledge-hammer to crack that nut. He'll wake up soon enough. Maybe it'll improve his manners, but I doubt it.'

'You hit him very hard.'

'He asked for it, didn't he?'

'Oh, yes, he provoked you. I'm not saying you weren't justified, but — '

'But what, Mr Walsh?'

Walsh looked uncomfortable. He lowered his voice. 'Is it altogether wise to antagonize these men? They have the advantage of numbers. Suppose they were to seize control.'

Barlow walked out of the cave and Walsh followed him. The sun was shining after the storm and steam was rising from the ground like smoke. The smell of rain was strong in the air.

'You think we should throw the women to them to appease their carnal appetites?' Barlow asked.

'I didn't say that,' Walsh protested. 'But it might be advisable to be more circumspect.'

Barlow snapped his fingers. 'The only way to be circumspect with a man like Fryer is to slam him down every time he tries to get up too high. Believe me, Mr Walsh, I know. I've had a load of Fryers to

175

deal with in my time. You can't treat them with the gentle touch. If you do, they think you're a weakling and they take advantage. The only thing those jokers respect is the hammer. You've got to hammer them; you've got to hammer them hard and often.'

'You think you've settled Fryer then?'

'I don't think I've settled him,' Barlow said. 'You never settle a man like that until you nail down the lid of the coffin. He'll try to get back at me and I'll have to watch him. But I'd have had to do that anyway.'

'I hope you know what you're doing.'

'If I don't know,' Barlow said, 'then I'm damned sure nobody else does.'

★　★　★

When Walsh left him Barlow continued walking. He wanted to think. But he had not gone far when he heard the scamper of feet behind him and he turned to see Katherine Summers.

'What's the hurry?' he asked.

She was panting a little. 'You've had trouble, Chris.'

'What trouble would that be?'

'Fryer. You hit him.'

'Sure I hit him. Has he waked up?'

'He says he's going to get you.'

'Never mind what he says. He'll make a lot of noise but he won't do anything. You don't need to worry your head about Ben Fryer.'

She was silent for a while as they walked along the shore with the sea foaming up over their bare feet. Then she said: 'Evelyn Partridge says there's bound to be an explosion before long. She says the men will start something.'

Barlow looked at her. 'Are you afraid?'

'Yes,' she admitted. 'But not as much as I was when you were away. You won't go away again, will you?'

'If I do,' he said, 'I'll take you with me.'

★ ★ ★

It was Katherine who saw it first. It was lying a few yards off-shore and the waves were breaking over it. One moment it would be submerged and the next moment it would jut up like a black rock.

177

'Look!' She pointed and Barlow followed the direction with his eyes. 'Over there. Can you see it?'

'I can see it,' he said.

'What is it?'

'Jetsam.'

He was already wading into the water, making his way towards the object. The girl held her skirt high and followed. When the water came up to her thighs she stopped and watched Barlow.

The bottom was firm under his feet; the water came up under his armpits and then dropped to his waist. He reached the jetsam and rested his hand on it. Spray flew over his head, drenching him.

He shouted to the girl: 'It's a cask.'

It was lying on its side. The timber had gathered some limpets and a thin beard of weed, but as far as Barlow could judge it was sound and unbroken. He got behind the cask and pushed; with the sea helping him he was able to move it with little difficulty. He began to roll it towards the shore, and when he had moved it a short way Katherine added her help. Together they pushed it clear of the water.

'It's heavy,' Katherine said.

'It's full. You can see the ends haven't been damaged. Could have come from a wreck. Could have been jettisoned.'

'What do you think is in it?'

'Wine. Maybe brandy.'

'Do you think it'll still be good?'

The staves of the cask had begun to steam in the sun. Barlow drummed his fingers on them. 'The cask hasn't been damaged. If it keeps the liquor in I'd say it'll keep sea-water out.'

'I wish we hadn't found it.'

He looked at her in surprise. 'Why?'

'Suppose those men get drunk. They're bad enough sober.'

'Nobody's going to get drunk. King will see to that.'

★ ★ ★

Mr King himself supervised the bringing in of the cask. He knew his men.

Fryer looked at it longingly. 'Good liquor in there. We could all do with a wet.'

'There'll be no drinking,' King said.

179

'The cask will be stored in my cave.'

'Have a heart,' Fryer said. 'All this work and not even a sip?'

'You heard my orders.'

Grimes tugged at Fryer's arm. 'Leave it, Ben.' He lowered his voice so that King could not hear. 'There's ways and means, Ben, ways and means. Lend a hand on the shoving now, there's the boy.'

Fryer lent a hand. There was sense in what Grimes had said. The cask might be stored in King's own cave, but there were certainly ways and means.

'You find any more stuff like this,' Fryer said to Barlow, 'just let me know. We'll share it fifty-fifty. Keep Mr King out of it.' He was affable now; he seemed to have forgotten all about the knock on the head. But Barlow was not deceived; a man like Benjamin Fryer did not forget an injury as easily as that. He would nurse his resentment and bring it out at a time and place to suit himself. He would still need watching.

★ ★ ★

180

The cask stood in the innermost part of the cave that King had made his own. Here King kept the boat-hook, the oars, the medicine chest and various other treasures that had been brought ashore from the wreck of the boat.

He kept the boat-hook under his own care, for with its sharp iron spike it was an offensive weapon, and he believed in keeping all offensive weapons under his control. True, the men had their knives, but it would have been out of the question to take these away from them, since they were needed for a hundred different tasks. But he had his revolver and a watchful eye, and he did not believe that any of these creatures, whom in his heart he despised, could succeed in taking him by surprise.

Fryer waited until the small hours of the morning to make his move. For so heavy a man he could tread surprisingly lightly when the occasion demanded. He paused outside King's cave in the moonlight and slid his long seaman's knife from its sheath. He gripped it in his right hand and went into the cave, softly, with

181

the stealth of a man who has murder in his heart.

He could not see anything inside the cave. Except for the first few yards within the entrance, all was black and silent. He paused, straining his ears to catch the sound of King's breathing. He could hear nothing but the faint mumble of the sea. But for himself the cave might well have been empty.

He wondered whether King had gone out. You could never tell with that devil; he had his whims and it was quite possible that he had got up and gone for a moonlight walk. Why any man should wish to go out walking in the middle of the night was more than Fryer could understand; but King was not a man you could understand; he was King.

Fryer began to feel uneasy. There ought to have been some sound in the darkness, but there was nothing. His eyes gradually becoming accustomed to the gloom, were able to probe a little farther into the cave. He fancied he could see some object lying on the ground, but he could not be certain. Perhaps it was King, perhaps not.

He took a hesitant step forward and made a crunching sound with his feet, as though he had stepped upon sea-shells.

He stopped again, his heart beating rapidly, and he could feel the sweat pricking out on his forehead. Suppose King should in fact be outside the cave; suppose he should come back and find the intruder. What would he do? Fryer could imagine only too well. He remembered Copley. King was far too quick and far too deadly with the revolver. He was a devil.

Fryer began to retreat. But then he halted again. It was ridiculous to go back now. King must be in there and he must be asleep. One quick thrust of the knife and there would be an end to the rule of Matthew King; one stab of the long sharp knife and then would begin the reign of Benjamin Fryer; and then, boys, get ready for the fun.

The thought hardened his resolve. He moved forward again into the shadow of the cave.

The dark shape lying on the floor did not move, and he knew that this was his man, that there could be no mistake. He gripped the knife firmly in his hand and struck suddenly, fiercely downward.

'That for you, bastard!'

The shock jarred his wrist. The blade of the knife passed through a bundle of dried seaweed and came into hard contact with the floor of the cave. It was the surprise of it more than the pain in his wrist that shook Fryer and brought a curse from his lips.

Then he heard King's voice coming from the deeper darkness: 'Stay just where you are, Fryer. Don't move or by heaven I'll put a bullet through your head.'

Fryer did not move. He knew that he must be presenting a clear target for King, outlined as he was against the moonlit entrance of the cave; and he knew King's skill with the gun.

King's tone became conversational, almost playful. 'Tell me, Fryer, can you suggest one valid reason why I should not put an end to your worthless existence as you would have put an end to mine?'

Fryer said hoarsely: 'You wouldn't do that, Mr King. I ain't done you no harm.'

'You have merely attempted to kill me.

Since you have failed, you plead that you have done me no harm. It is not your fault that you have not. You struck very hard, Fryer, very hard indeed. Perhaps you have even hurt your own hand.'

Fryer's mouth was dry. He tried to swallow. His voice was a croak. 'Don't play with me, Mr King. You got the drop on me all right. But you don't have to kill me. I swear this won't never happen again. I swear it. You can trust me.'

'I'd sooner trust a rattlesnake.'

Fryer tried to see into the darkness. He could hear King's voice but could not see him. He felt as exposed as a man caught in the beam of a searchlight. At any moment a bullet might come blasting out of that darkness to smash into his head.

Suppose he were to dive to the ground; suppose he were to make a sudden rush at King. He did neither; he knew that neither course of action could hold any hope of success. King had all the time in the world to shoot him, for he was blind and King had eyes.

The harsh voice came again out of the darkness. 'I suppose you thought to set yourself up in my place — Caliban for Prospero. Forget it, Fryer; you haven't the brains.'

'You're right, Mr King; you're dead right,' Fryer said desperately. 'I ain't got the savvy to set meself up against you, sir; so you don't need to trouble yourself to kill me.'

'No trouble, Fryer; no trouble, I assure you.'

Fryer stumbled on. 'You let me go and I won't be no worry to you. You kill me and you just lose a good man. I catch fish, don't I? I do my work. You don't want to lose a man what works hard. Might come a time when you'd be sorry you didn't have a man like me. You kill me and you can't never bring me to life no more; it's done with, finished. You don't have to kill me, Mr King, not me. I'll do whatever you say. I'll keep them others on your side too. I'll see that there Grimes don't sneak up on you.'

He stopped speaking. He was panting. He peered again into the darkness. King made no answer and the sweat was pouring down Fryer's back.

'For Christ's sake, Mr King,' he burst out, 'say something. Don't keep me dangling on the hook like this.' He was almost sobbing.

'Interesting,' King said. 'The breakdown of the man of violence under the threat of imminent destruction.' He was like a scientist noting the result of some experiment. There was a cold, clinical quality about his voice which made Fryer even more fearful. He could have faced rage and bluster far more easily than this complete lack of emotion.

'You wouldn't shoot me,' Fryer mumbled; but there was no conviction in the words.

The crack of the revolver echoed loudly in the cave, the rocky walls flinging back the sound, flame spurting redly and then dying.

Fryer lay flat on his stomach and wondered why he was not dead. He waited for a second shot, his limbs paralysed with fear, his fingers digging into the floor of the cave. He heard King's voice again, still perfectly calm, perfectly controlled.

187

'You may go now. I have given you a warning, that is all. The time has not yet come when it may be necessary for me to kill you. But be warned.'

Fryer's whole body was shaking. 'Mad,' he muttered. 'Mad as they come.'

King's voice rose slightly. 'I said go.'

Fryer got up and went out of the cave, feeling exposed, naked, waiting for the bullet in the back. None came. When he was clear of the cave he began to let obscenities fall from his mouth like vomit. He would get even with King for this, see if he didn't.

14

Big Fish

Evelyn Partridge could smell the fish twenty yards away. Lynch was gutting them with his knife and hanging them on a thin bamboo rod supported by two crutched stakes. The sun beat down upon them, drying them.

'You know what I'd like?' Lynch said, squinting up at the stewardess. 'A nice crust of dry bread. Fish an' coconut an' fruit; fruit an' fish an' coconut: there's a diet.'

'You'll be able to have all the dry bread you want when we get away from here,' Miss Partridge said.

Lynch shook his head. 'We ain't getting away from here though. Not never. We're here for keeps. We're here till we all go barmy like some has done already. It's a bright future and no mistake.'

Miss Partridge walked away from him

down towards the beach. A bright future! Suppose Lynch were right; suppose they never did get away. And even if they did, what kind of a future was there for her? The same sort of job, year after year, until she became too old to do it; then retirement, scraping and scrounging to make ends meet. A bright future indeed.

★   ★   ★

Barlow was honing his knife on a piece of rock. He wetted the rock with water from a coconut shell and moved the blade rhythmically.

Walsh came and watched him. 'Sharpening that knife for any special purpose, bosun?'

Barlow nodded. 'A very special purpose.'

Walsh squatted down in his ragged pyjamas and the vivid dressing-gown. He looked tired, as though he had not been sleeping well; there were heavy pouches under his eyes.

'I hope you're not thinking of killing anyone,' he said anxiously.

'Why? Think it might be you?'

Walsh was serious. 'No, not me. There's no reason why you should want to kill me. I'm harmless.'

'Who then?'

'I'd rather not mention names.'

'You shouldn't let it worry you.'

'But it does worry me,' Walsh said earnestly. 'I told you before, I hate killing. And there's been too much death already. God knows where it will stop.'

'Well, you can put your mind at rest about this knife,' Barlow said. 'I'm not getting it ready to kill anyone. I've got quite a different purpose in view.'

Walsh appeared relieved. 'I'm glad to hear it. What sort of purpose?'

'Stick around and you'll see.'

Barlow tested the edge of the blade on the ball of his thumb and decided that it was as sharp as he could hope to make it. He soaked his beard in water and began to shave, using the knife as a razor. Walsh looked on with interest.

'I hadn't thought of that.'

It was not a good shave; the knife was no razor; but it made him feel cleaner.

Meade came past, carrying fish-hooks and lines. He paused in front of Barlow.

'Shaving saloon, eh?'

'That's right,' Barlow said. 'Want me to operate on you?'

Meade grinned. 'No, thanks. Operate might be the right word.' He stroked the golden hair on his chin. 'Besides, I rather like this beard.'

Barlow had to admit that the beard did something for Meade; it gave him the look of a Viking. Meade, stripped down to a pair of trousers, was all one colour from the waist upward — a golden brown. Barlow could understand why Helen Tudor was in love with him; Meade could have passed as any girl's dream man, and the beard added the final touch of glamour.

Meade said: 'I'm going to catch some fish. I'm going to catch me the biggest fish you ever saw.'

'I've seen whales.'

'Right then. I'll catch a whale. Ah, why be mean? Make it two whales.'

He walked off towards the beach with the easy, elastic movement of the athlete.

Watching him, Walsh felt a prick of envy and a disgust with his own body that was so soft and flabby and aging. Yet once he had been as fit as Meade. At Meade's age he had not had an ounce of fat on him and he had been able to shove his weight in the scrum with the best of them. But he had let himself go; he knew that. The business had claimed him, and he had stopped taking exercise and had eaten far more than his body needed. So the body, as if in protest, had degenerated; and now it was too late to do anything about it. He sighed. He would never again be like Arnold Meade.

'Something worrying you?' Barlow asked.

Walsh shook his head. 'No, nothing, nothing.'

★ ★ ★

Meade reached the sea and went on round the wide curve of the shore, heading for the point where the stream ran down from the higher ground.

He had walked about half a mile when

he came upon Helen Tudor asleep behind a rock. He stirred her with his foot and she awoke and stared up at him in the hot sunlight.

'Tired?' he asked. 'Not getting sleep at nights?'

She sat up, shaking the sand out of her hair. 'I must have dozed off. It's that kind of climate.'

Meade dropped the fish-hooks and crouched down beside her. She was yawning, still only half awake.

'Why did you come all this way out?' he asked.

'I wanted to think.'

'And that's what sent you to sleep? The effort. What did you think about?'

'It wouldn't interest you.'

'Maybe it would.'

'And maybe I'll tell you some time.'

'That's a promise.' He took her hand. 'Come for a swim. Wash the sleep away.'

She allowed him to pull her to her feet. Today he seemed to be in a cheerful mood and she was pleased to see him so happy. Perhaps for the moment he had forgotten about his future and was content to accept things as they were, to enjoy the simple pleasure of being alive.

She said: 'What a man you are, Arnold. Were you ever in love?'

He kissed her. 'I'm in love with you. Didn't I tell you?'

'I've forgotten. Tell me again.'

'I love you.' He kissed her again. 'Now let's have that swim.'

They stripped and raced naked to the sea, their feet scattering sand. They ran hand in hand like children, laughing. It was as though they were alone in the world, as though the world were young and fresh and lovely. Helen Tudor shut out of her mind all misgivings, all doubts, all fears; she let the years slip like a discarded cloak from her smooth bare shoulders, reaching back into her youth.

The sea came to meet them in small rippling waves that lapped their bodies as they plunged deeper and deeper. It touched their knees, their waists, their armpits. They began to swim, side by side, stroke for stroke, moving easily through the tepid water, out towards the emptiness beyond the land.

They stopped swimming and looked back towards the beach. They could see a small figure moving in the distance; it was so far away that there was a sense of unreality about it. It seemed as though they had cut themselves off from the world and could never go back to it.

Meade said: 'No need to worry about the neighbours here. No beach regulations.'

'Only those King makes.'

She immediately regretted saying that. The thought of King was an unwelcome intrusion into this private Eden of herself and Meade.

'King doesn't rule out here,' Meade said. He rolled over and gave a thrust with his legs, pushing himself towards her. He put his arms about her, and his mouth was on hers, and she could taste the salt. They went under, still locked together. They came up gasping for air and lay on the surface, floating, with the sun beating down on them.

Helen closed her eyes and let the sea hold her. It was a gentle hold; it lifted her, let her fall again, with a sleepy, rhythmic motion. It would be easy to fall asleep, perhaps too easy.

She heard Meade's voice again. 'Hey, wake up. What a girl you are for dozing.'

She opened her eyes and saw him turn over in a dive. He disappeared, but a moment later she felt him come up beneath her; and then his arms were round her again. She struggled to free herself; it was a game; but she could not loose his arms; he was too strong. He dragged her under and held her there until her lungs were burning, and she wondered in momentary panic whether he really meant to kill her. Then he released her and they both shot to the surface and the air came sobbing back into her body. 'You nearly drowned me,' she said accusingly. 'Were you trying to?'

Meade grinned. 'You know I wouldn't want to drown you. This would be a hell of a dull place without you.'

'It would be dull for me without you, Arnold. Worse. If you weren't here I don't think I'd want to live any more.'

'Sure you would. I'm not that important to you.'

'You don't know how important,' she said; but he was not listening to her; he was swimming away, farther out to sea, with long, powerful strokes. He was a fine swimmer.

She did not follow him. Suddenly she had become afraid of the sea, of its vastness, stretching away to the horizon, stretching away beneath her. She felt caught by it; it was no longer a gentle lover holding her in its arms; it was a monster that had seized her and perhaps would never let her go.

She shouted to Meade: 'I'm going back.' But he was a long way off and might not have heard.

She began to swim towards the land with feverish, desperate energy. It seemed very far away. The energy burnt itself out and she felt wretchedly tired, her arms and legs became leaden; and still the beach was far away, apparently coming no nearer.

She looked for Meade and could not see him. She needed his help now and he was not there to give it. A fear of drowning possessed her, and in a sudden panic she began to beat at the sea with her hands and feet, as though in that way she would drive it from her. But the sea was not driven away; it closed over her head and salt water went into her mouth and stung her throat. She could see now only a kind of subdued, greenish light that seemed to ripple, forming strange and horrible shapes, illusions of clutching hands and leering faces.

Helen Tudor came to the surface and made an effort of will to conquer her panic. 'Don't be a fool. There's no danger. Just swim slowly and calmly.'

Her arms and legs were still weary but she managed to get the stroke going. The panic faded; the beach drew nearer.

'You see; you see. There was nothing to be afraid of, nothing at all.'

But she was thankful to feel the sand under her feet, and it was a relief to lie there letting the sun dry the water from her skin, just to lie there doing nothing, waiting for the strength to flow back into her body.

It was Meade's scream that roused her. In her own struggle she had forgotten him. Now she sat up in sudden concern and looked at the sea, searching for him.

Her gaze found him almost at once, and she knew then why he had screamed. She saw the angry churning of the water; she saw the sharp fin; she heard Meade scream again, but only once.

She could not move; it was as though her whole body had been turned to stone. She watched until it was finished, until there was nothing more to watch. And even then she still crouched there, staring out across the calm, blue surface of the sea where Meade had been.

15

Overthrow

King sat on his chair of state within the semi-circle of grinning skulls.

'I am not satisfied,' he said.

The others stood in two groups, facing him. In one group were Fryer, Grimes, Lynch and McKay; in the other were Barlow, Walsh and the three women.

Helen Tudor looked haggard; there were dark patches under her eyes. In one night she seemed to have lost all the sparkle of life; it was as if twenty years had laid their burden upon her shoulders in the moment when Meade had died.

Katherine Summers had tried to comfort her, but without success.

'I loved him. And now he's gone. You can't understand what that means.'

'Perhaps I can.'

'I loved him. He never really loved me. I know that. It didn't make any difference. I loved him and the sea took him. I hate the sea.'

Helen Tudor's hair was bedraggled; it was sticky with salt and there was sand in it. She had ceased to care about her appearance.

Walsh tugged at the cord of his dressing-gown. He spoke nervously. 'Not satisfied with what, Mr King?'

'With your conduct — the conduct of all of you. Things have become slack; there has been a lack of discipline; I have been too lenient. There has been too much independent action, each one for himself, ignoring the good of the community. That has got to stop. In future we work to a routine. There will be a muster at sunrise each morning.'

'T'hell wi' that for a game,' McKay muttered.

King's gaze switched to him; anger in his eyes. 'What did you say? Speak up, man. Don't keep it to yourself. Let us all have the benefit of your pearls of wisdom.'

McKay stared at the ground; he could not face King's eyes. He shuffled his feet, mumbling: 'I didna say anything.'

'Very well,' King said. 'I will continue. There will be a muster each morning. Anyone absent will be punished. At muster I shall allot your tasks for the day, and I will see that those tasks are carried out. There will be no more slacking.'

Grimes looked at King, his face sharp, his mouth twisted into the suggestion of a grin. He had his knife in his right hand and he was paring the nails of the left hand, scraping under them with the point of the blade. Grimes's knife had a bone handle and a thin, tapering blade. He spent a lot of time sharpening it, spitting on the stone and rubbing, rubbing, rubbing. Grimes often remarked that a sharp knife was a seaman's best friend. There were a lot of things you could do with a good knife, and paring your nails was only one of them.

'No more slacking,' Grimes said. 'That's right, Mr King. There's some here what never did pull their weight. Too high and mighty maybe. No names, no pack-drill, as the saying is. But no slacking — that's telling 'em; that's putting it straight, as the ruler said to pencil.'

'I didn't ask for your opinion,' King said acidly. 'I am not interested in what you think.'

Grimes was busy with his knife, not looking at King now, intent on the task in hand. He seemed to be grinning to himself — slyly.

'Not interested, eh? Well, of course not. I ain't much beside a man like you, am I? I'm just dirt, ain't I? All right, so I'm dirt.'

'Stow it, Bart,' Fryer said. 'You talk too much. You be quiet and listen to what Mr King has to say.'

'I'm listening,' Grimes said. He winked at Fryer and rubbed the handle of the knife on his chin. 'I'm listening.'

King said: 'It will not have escaped your notice that since our arrival here our numbers have been gradually falling. First there was Lanyon, then Copley, now Meade.'

'Ten left,' Grimes said. 'Ten little nigger boys.'

Lynch shuffled his feet. Lynch had very big feet; they were out of proportion to his thin, spindly legs. He had become thinner and his face looked yellow; it was as

204

though some disease were slowly wasting him away. Perhaps it was the venom feeding on his flesh, for Lynch was a venomous man.

'It's this place,' he said. 'There's a curse on it. Maybe it's them up there.' He made a gesture towards the mountain. 'Maybe it's them idols what the bosun found. Maybe it's them what's killing us one by one — them gods.'

King glowered at Lynch. 'They are not gods. There are no gods here. Do not talk to me of gods.'

Lynch pulled at his lower lip. 'There's a curse anyways. Else why's there three dead?'

'The curse is idleness,' King said. 'Work is the answer to all our problems. I intend to make you work — all of you.'

Barlow watched King, observing him closely for signs of mental unbalance. King talked so lucidly that it was difficult to believe he could be mad. And yet he must be; there could be no other explanation for his actions. Nevertheless, it was a clear-headed madness; he was watchful and wary. Fryer had tried to kill him and had failed.

Barlow wondered whether King ever slept. If he did, it must have been a sleep so light that he was ready to wake in a moment with his hand on the gun, that ultimate authority. If he ever lost the gun things would be different, very different. But they might be far worse.

'Mr King,' Fryer said suddenly. His voice was hoarse and he was sweating heavily. 'I believe you are a good shot.'

King looked at Fryer. 'Well?'

'I just wondered how good.'

Barlow glanced sharply at Fryer. There was something at the back of this. Fryer was not simply making idle conversation; there was some plan in his mind. Barlow wondered whether Fryer had thought out the plan or whether it had been another, sharper brain that had forged it.

Grimes was still paring his nails with the knife; he seemed to be interested only in that operation, but his eyes were watchful, missing nothing.

'You wondered how good, eh?' King said thoughtfully. 'The question interests you?'

Fryer's voice was a croak; the words seemed to be forced out of him. 'Seems to me with a revolver it'd take a good man to be all that accurate. To be sure of hitting a target, if you get me.'

'I get you, Fryer.'

King's hand dropped to the butt of the revolver. He pulled it out of his belt and held it loosely, not pointing it at Fryer, not pointing it at anyone, but letting it rest lightly in the grip of his right hand.

'I could hit you, Fryer.'

'Oh, yes, sure you could. But I'm a big target. That wouldn't be no achievement, not hitting me wouldn't.'

The sweat was running down Fryer's forehead; an oily drop hung on the end of his nose.

'Quite right, Fryer,' King said. 'You are a very big target. Even a poor marksman could hit you.' As though absent-mindedly he pulled back the hammer with his thumb and lifted the barrel of the revolver until it was pointing at Fryer's ample stomach.

Fryer stared at the revolver, fascinated by it; but the words came from him automatically, like a speech learned by heart.

'I saw a bloke in a circus once. He could use a revolver. I saw him light a match at twenty yards with one shot. He was good.'

King was listening. He was interested. It was apparent in his face. His head was cocked slightly on one side and his eyes were watching Fryer keenly.

'I never saw nobody else that good,' Fryer said. 'Don't reckon there is anybody. He was one by himself — the top.'

'Nonsense,' King said.

Fryer looked surprised. 'You don't think I saw him do it? You can be sure I did, sir. I saw him sure enough with my own two eyes.'

King put the forefinger of his left hand on the barrel of the revolver and slid it towards the foresight and back again.

'I don't disbelieve you. But it is nonsense to suggest that no one else could do as much as the man you saw. I could do it myself.'

'You could, sir?' Fryer's voice had lost some of its hoarseness. He seemed to be gaining confidence. 'I'd like to see that.' He put a hand in his pocket and pulled out a small white sliver of wood. 'I got a match here. It's a dead one, so you won't be able to light it. But I'd like to see you hit it at twenty paces. Yes, I'd like to see that.'

'Will you hold it?'

Fryer laughed, but the laughter had a hint of uneasiness in it. 'Mr King, you wouldn't expect me to do that. That'd be asking too much.'

King asked with deceptive mildness: 'Have you no faith in my ability?'

'Oh, sure, sure,' Fryer said. 'I have faith in you. But it's like this — my hand might shake. It'd take a bit of nerve to stand there like William Tell's kid. I reckon there ain't a man here what'd take that on.'

'The boy had courage. You have none.' King's voice hardened. 'Hold the match.'

Fryer's lips quivered and the sweat blinded him. 'Mr King, you don't mean that. I'll stick it in the ground; you can shoot at it there.'

King's face was like iron; there was no hint of mercy in it. 'If you refuse to hold the match I will shoot you in the belly. Perhaps that will teach you not to goad me with tales of circus performers. Now will you do it?'

'I can't, sir. God's truth, I can't.'

King's index finger curled about the trigger of the revolver. 'I'll give you five seconds.' He began to count. 'One — two — '

Lynch and McKay edged away from Fryer, shifting out of the line of fire.

Walsh shouted: 'You can't do this, King. Good God, man, you can't do it.'

King's voice did not falter. 'Three — four — '

The revolver was pointed at Fryer's stomach. He gave in.

'All right, Mr King, I'll do it. You don't have to shoot me. I'll do what you say. But for Christ's sake, shoot straight.'

He moved away to the right, stumbling, as though he were slightly drunk. He did not walk twenty paces; he halted some ten yards away from King and held the match in his left hand, stretching out his arm to its full extent.

King turned on his seat and brought the

revolver up slowly. King's hand was steady, but Fryer's hand was shaking; he could not hold the match still.

'You make my task more difficult,' King said; and even as he spoke he fired.

Fryer's scream came like an echo of the report of the gun. Barlow saw the finger and thumb that had been holding the match suddenly mangled and bleeding. It had been good shooting, but not quite perfect.

Then he saw Fryer rush forward, yelling with rage and pain, and he expected to hear again the crack of the revolver, to see Fryer stopped in his tracks. But no shots came; and then Fryer was inside the crescent of skulls, and Barlow saw why the revolver had not stopped him, why it could not stop him.

King was lying face downward on the ground with the revolver a few feet away from him. King was twitching, but he was making no sound. Grimes was looking down at him and grinning. There was a knife in King's back, and it was the knife that Grimes had been using to pare his nails. He had found another use for it now.

Fryer stopped yelling. He stood and picked up the revolver with his right hand. He pointed it at King and fired until the cylinder was empty. One bullet struck the base of King's skull, one went into his shoulder, and the others missed, scattering little spurts of dust as they ploughed into the ground.

Fryer dangled the revolver in his right hand and began to kick King's lifeless body, cursing it and spitting on it.

'That for you, you bastard! Who's boss now? So you'd shoot my hand, would you. Well, you won't shoot nothing else. You thought you was clever, but you weren't clever enough for me and little Bartie, not by a long chalk.'

He stopped kicking King's body and looked down at his left hand. The blood had dripped on to his trousers, leaving a long red stain down the side of his leg.

'Damn him,' Fryer said. 'Why couldn't he shoot straight?'

Grimes said with his cunning smile: 'He didn't do so bad at that. He got pretty close to the mark. Some people might have aimed for the finger and scored a bull's-eye in the guts. Maybe you was lucky.'

'Lucky! With this?' Fryer held up the maimed hand, pain contorting his face. 'That's easy for you to say. You had the cushy part. You didn't have to stand up in front of a raving maniac with a gun.'

'No,' Grimes said. 'But I killed him, didn't I?' He bent down and wrenched the knife out of King's back. He wiped the blade perfunctorily on King's clothing and slipped it back in its sheath. He looked round at the others, noting the various expressions on their faces, the horror on some, the satisfaction on others.

'It's a different set-up now,' he said.

The tic was visible in Walsh's cheek; the whole of one side of his face seemed to be leaping and quivering; and his hands were shaking. Katherine had turned away and been sick; Helen Tudor looked drugged, her eyes glassy; McKay and Lynch were grinning.

Barlow was blaming himself for not having kept an eye on Grimes. He, like everyone else, had been watching the demonstration of shooting, and Grimes had been able to sneak round behind King without being observed. When Barlow had seen him it had been too late; but he blamed himself. It was certainly a different set-up now, and he did not like it.

'That's right, Bartie,' Fryer said. 'You tell 'em. Tell 'em who's in charge now. Tell 'em who's boss.'

'Why, you, Ben,' Grimes said, winking and leering like a small, animated gargoyle. 'You and nobody else. You got the gun.'

'By God, you're right. I got the gun. You hear that, bosun?'

'I hear it,' Barlow said.

'Remember it then.'

'He won't get the chance to forget,' Grimes said. 'We'll keep it in his mind, won't we, Ben? No more being kicked around by a bloody bosun. We got him where we want him now, eh, Ben? Just where we want him.'

'Stow your gab,' Fryer said. 'I'll do the talking.'

Grimes winked and grimaced; he

seemed unable to contain his delight. 'Just as you say, Ben. You're the boss.'

Fryer turned to Evelyn Partridge. 'Hey, you. Fetch the medicine chest and tie this ruddy hand up afore I bleed to death.'

Miss Partridge said coldly: 'You don't deserve any medical attention.'

'Never mind what I deserve. You do as I say. Got it?'

'I understand you perfectly.'

'Move then.'

Miss Partridge turned and walked towards the cave that King had occupied and now would need no more. She walked without haste, very stiff and upright. When she returned she was carrying the first-aid box that had been salvaged from the lifeboat. She set to work with professional skill on bandaging the damaged hand, while Barlow, Walsh, McKay and Lynch, in obedience to Fryer's orders, carried King's body away for burial.

'You don't need to read no funeral service over him,' Fryer said. 'Just dig a hole and kick the bastard in. Take his clothes off first though. We can use them.'

Miss Partridge said: 'I suppose you realize you may lose your arm.'

Fryer stared at her, his jaw sagging. 'What you mean — lose my arm?'

'Blood poison. Gangrene.' She enunciated the words with a certain relish. 'Those fingers ought to be amputated.'

'Nobody's going to cut my fingers off.'

'Better the fingers than the whole arm.'

'You think it might come to that?' Fryer's voice had lost its bluster. He peered into Miss Partridge's face, trying to read the truth there.

'I'm not a doctor,' she said.

'You know about nursing though. You had training.'

'Some.'

'Well, then — '

'I can only tell you what might happen. Blood poison could travel up the arm. If it gets to the heart, that's the end. It might be better to have the fingers off at once. Mr Grimes has a sharp knife.'

Grimes was leering. 'That's right. I'd do it. I ain't no surgeon, mind, but I'd have a go for a pal.' He pulled the knife, still stained with King's blood, out of its sheath and fingered the blade. 'It's sharp Ben, sharp as a razor. Or a scalpel. You won't hardly feel it.'

Fryer was sweating again. There was a pain in his hand and the pain seemed to be creeping up his arm. Perhaps it was the poison already moving through his blood stream.

'Better have the finger off,' Grimes said softly. 'Or maybe I should've said thumb and finger to be correct.' He twisted the knife in his hand fondly, as though eager to begin. 'Maybe I should've been a surgeon.'

'You keep that knife off of me,' Fryer said. 'I ain't going to be carved up by you nor nobody.'

Grimes looked disappointed. 'Better the fingers than the arm. You heard what the lady said. I mightn't make such a good job of the arm. More to get through. Need a saw.'

'I ain't going to lose my arm and I ain't going to lose my fingers neither,' Fryer shouted. 'So you can put that knife away and forget about it.'

Grimes shrugged. 'It's your funeral.'

He put the knife back in its sheath and began to whistle tunelessly.

Miss Partridge went on with the bandaging. They could hear the others scooping out a grave for the dead man.

16

New Order

The fire leaped and danced like a demon. It was a red spear piercing the darkness, red and bloody. It threw a baleful light on the faces of those who were gathered round it. In the distance the sea could be heard falling on the beach with its timeless, endless dirge. Inland lay the darkness, the unknown, the three carved idols and the ghosts of the dead.

Fryer was sitting on the chair of state with his shirt open to the waist and his trousers stretched tightly over his bulging thighs. The firelight glowed on his bearded face and the round, sun-tanned dome of his head. The revolver was thrust ostentatiously in his leather belt and there were rounds in the cylinder.

Fryer had taken over the cave that King had used, and with the cave he had taken possession of the stores that were there, including the ammunition for the revolver.

Fryer was in command now and Grimes was his lieutenant, the sly courtier, the whisperer in the ear, the finger on the pulse. Grimes was content to let Fryer have all the outward show of power as long as he was the brain behind the dictator, as long as he could manipulate the strings of the puppet without the puppet's realizing that there were any strings to manipulate.

'Tonight,' Grimes had said, 'I reckon we ought to celebrate. The King is dead. Long live the King.'

'You're right; we'll celebrate,' Fryer had said. 'We been long enough without any fun and games. We been oppressed, that's what we been, oppressed. Well, boy, if there's to be any more of that it'll be a different oppressor. What you say?'

'I say right, Ben; right in one.'

Some of the blood had seeped through the bandage on Fryer's left hand. He could feel the hand throbbing. He tried not to think about blood poisoning.

The cask was standing close to Fryer's

right hand. They had rolled it out of the cave and had knocked a hole in the top. They had smelt the rich odour breathing out of it, giving promise of bacchanalian pleasures to come, of drunkenness and revelry.

'Rum!'

The rum was dark and strong. Grimes doled it out in generous measures. The cups were the hollow halves of coconut shells, rubbed smooth with sand, and the rum was the first liquor that the men had had for weeks.

From beyond the circle of the firelight Walsh and Barlow watched the others drinking.

'What do you think they'll do when they get really drunk?' Walsh asked nervously.

'They may just go to sleep,' Barlow said. 'Or they may get other ideas.' He glanced towards the group of women standing a short way off.

Walsh noted the direction of the glance. 'It would have been better if King had stayed alive. At least he kept them in check.'

'King knew better than to let them get at the rum. But there'll be no stopping them now.'

They heard Fryer give a sudden shout. 'Where's the rest of the party? Where's that bosun? Hey, Barlow!'

'I'm here,' Barlow said.

'Well, come and drink, damn you. You ain't teetotal, are you? Never knew a bosun that was. Or are you too bloody high and mighty to take a drink with the lads?'

'Better go,' Barlow said to Walsh. 'Better humour the bastard.'

The two of them walked into the firelight and Fryer saw them appear out of the encircling darkness.

'So there you are, and Mr Walsh too. What you been holding back for? Can't you take a shot of rum? Or ain't the company good enough?'

'We'll drink if it's free,' Barlow said.

Walsh added: 'Yes, certainly. A drink would be very pleasant. Haven't tasted rum for quite some time.'

'Taste!' Fryer said. 'You'll do more than taste. You'll have a right good swill. You'll drown your bleedin' guts in it. This is liberty hall; there's plenty for everybody — even bosuns and flamin' passengers. Right, Bartie?'

'Right, Skipper,' Grimes said. He picked up two coconut shells, dipped them in the cask and handed one to Barlow and the other to Walsh.

Fryer lifted his own cup. 'To the prosperity and happiness of Fryer's Kingdom and all what sail in her. Amen.' His speech was beginning to slur, and when he put the shell to his lips some of the liquor ran over and trickled down his beard, dripping stickily on to his bare chest. He was half drunk already, and Lynch and McKay were in a similar condition. Only Grimes seemed to be unaffected by the rum. He stood with his hands on the cask, looking more wizened, more sly and weasel-like than ever, his eyes bright and beady in the firelight.

Barlow tipped his cup and the rum traced a fiery trail along his throat and down into his stomach. The fumes of it climbed into his brain.

Walsh said ingratiatingly: 'This is good

liquor, Mr Fryer.'

Fryer belched loudly. 'You bet it's good. We have none but the best in this house, none but the best.'

'But it won't last long,' Grimes said, peering into the cask as though he were measuring the quantity with his eye.

'To hell with lasting long,' Fryer said. 'We'll send the bosun to look for some more. We'll throw him in the sea and make him stay there till he's found another barrel. What you say to that, bose?'

'It might take a long time.'

'Who care if it takes till the Day of Judgement? Do what you're told, see? No back answers. Understand?'

'Sure I do,' Barlow said.

'Okay then, okay. If I say go into the sea, you go. If I say find some more rum, you find it. I'm boss here; me, Ben Fryer, nobody else.' He waved the shell, spilling rum. 'You all better get that into your thick skulls and save yourselves a lot of bother. Specially you, bose, specially you.'

'The bosun's a nice boy,' Grimes said with the hint of a sneer. 'He knows how to behave himself. He won't make trouble.'

'He better not.'

Grimes winked at Barlow. He was enjoying himself. 'The Skipper here's going to change the laws. We're going to have a fresh start now he's in charge. The Skipper — '

'To hell with Skipper,' Fryer said. 'I'm more than that. I'm a sultan. Sultan Benjamin — that's me.'

'Sultan. Oh, that's a good one. Bow to his Royal Highness the Sultan Benjamin.'

Grimes bowed low. Lynch and McKay did the same. Barlow looked at Fryer but made no movement.

'The bosun ain't bowing.' Grimes said. 'Maybe he thinks he's too important. You oughter see about that, Sultan.'

Fryer threw the shell from which he had been drinking on the ground at Barlow's feet, scattering the last few drops of rum. His voice was thick with the sudden and unpredictable anger of the drunk.

'By God, I will see to it.' He hauled the revolver out of his belt and his finger curled about the trigger. The barrel wavered, pointing first at Barlow's stomach, then at his face. 'Bow to me, you bloody mutineer. Bow.'

'Do as he says,' Walsh said urgently. 'He'll shoot.'

Barlow bent at the waist, but he kept his eyes on the revolver.

'That's better,' Fryer said. 'I'll have no mutineers here.' He thrust the gun back in his belt and called for more rum. Grimes moved quickly to give it to him and Fryer gulped the neat spirit.

Suddenly a thought seemed to come into his head. 'The women! Where's them women got to? Why ain't they drinking?'

'Leave the women alone,' Barlow said.

Fryer glared at him. 'Who told you to speak? You speak when I give permission, see? And if I say let the women come and drink, they come.'

'They don't want to drink rum. It isn't a woman's drink.'

'Anything's a woman's drink. Did you ask 'em?'

'They won't drink rum,' Barlow said. 'Leave them alone.'

'Leave them alone, is it?' Fryer's eyes narrowed; he seemed to be trying to focus them through the fog of drunkenness. 'Maybe we left 'em alone too long. Maybe we left 'em to Mr Meade and Mr Walsh and Mr Barlow. Maybe now it's somebody else's turn.'

Barlow took a step forward and felt Walsh's hand on his arm, restraining him. 'Not now. It wouldn't do any good. Not now.' Walsh's voice had a nervous urgency.

Grimes said: 'I don't see why a nice well brought up lady shouldn't be partial to a drop of good rum. Ain't as if it was poison.'

'I'll have some,' Helen Tudor said, and stepped into the circle of firelight.

Walsh said hesitantly: 'I don't think this is quite the place for you, Miss Tudor.'

She gave him a long, cool stare, which disconcerted him. The fire had discovered reddish glints in her golden hair and all the men were gazing at her.

'What would be the place for me, Mr Walsh?' she said. 'Do you know? Does anyone know? Why not this place as well as any other?' She turned to Grimes. 'Gimme some of that stuff. God, I need a drink. I need a drink like I've never needed one before in all my life.'

Grimes said, grinning at her like a fox: 'One drink coming up, lady. No waiting at this bar. No paying neither. It's all on the house.'

He dipped a coconut cup in the cask and handed it to her, the rum almost level with the rim. She threw her head back and let the spirit run down her throat, trying to drown the misery that was in her, trying to burn out the memory.

'She can take it,' Fryer said. 'The lady can take her liquor.'

There was truth in what he said. She drained the cup and handed it back to Grimes.

'More.'

Grimes sniggered, nodding his head as if it had been mounted on a spiral spring. He dipped the shell and pulled it out, full again to the brim.

'There you are, lady; you just put that where the other went and there ain't no telling what might happen. You'll be lit up like a flaming fire.'

'You don't have to tell me,' Helen Tudor said. She took the cup and drank again, then gave a laugh, brief and bitter. 'We can all get dead drunk, can't we? Better drunk than dead. Some are just dead. Why aren't we all? God, why aren't we all?'

'We will be,' Grimes said. 'Some day. But not yet.'

She drank again, spilling some of the liquor. It ran down her chin and made a dark stain on her shirt. She was swaying slightly as the alcohol took effect. Grimes watched her with his beady eyes; Fryer watched her through the haze of his drunkenness; Lynch and McKay watched her also, waiting, expectant.

She gave a wide sweep of her arm. Rum splashed from the cup and some drops fell on the fire, which leaped up in a burst of flame, revived by the spirit.

'Why are you all staring at me?' she demanded. 'Why don't you say something? Lost your tongues? Why don't you sing, for Pete's sake?'

'You sing, sweetheart,' Fryer said. 'Sing like you used to in the night clubs. We heard about that. Maybe you can dance too.'

'Maybe I can.'

She took another drink from the shell and began to make sinuous movements with her body. She stumbled, but regained her balance. Grimes's bony fingers tapped a rhythm on the weathered timber of the cask. He had drunk as much as any man and it had had no apparent effect on him; he had lost none of his self-command, none of his sharpness. His hands were steady, the tapping fingers as controlled as a bandsman's drumsticks.

'Another drink, sister?'

He reached out and took the shell from her. In a moment it was back in her hand replenished.

'Give us the dance, sister.'

'That's right,' Fryer said. 'Show your legs, girlie. Show everything.'

Barlow stepped forward and touched Helen Tudor's arm. 'Why don't you come away? You've had enough.'

She freed herself from his hand, staggering. 'Enough! Can't ever have enough. Not ever.'

'It's time to go,' Barlow said.

'Leave her be,' Fryer shouted. 'You get to hell out of it, bosun. The lady likes it here. She likes the company. Don't you, sweetheart?'

'I hate the company,' she said. 'It's lousy. But I like the drink.' Her gaze fell on Barlow again. 'Why don't you go away?' She took a swipe at him with her hand, missed the target and fell on her knees. The men laughed.

'Why don't you sing?' she shouted. 'What's wrong with you? Sing, damn you.'

Fryer said: 'Maybe you start, hey? You're the singer. Give us a lead.'

She began to sing then. It was a mawkish pop song. The men knew it and joined in. Grimes took a skull from one of the stakes and beat out the time with it on the cask. The skull made a hollow drumming sound.

The woman's voice was thin and strangely childlike when she sang; it seemed to float above the deeper sound of the men's voices. Barlow retreated from the firelight and stood with Walsh beyond the edge of the flickering circle.

'I don't like this,' Walsh said. 'That woman's drunk.'

'They're all drunk.'

'Except Grimes.'

'He's drunk too, but he doesn't show it. He's the really dangerous sort. God keep me from the man who can be drunk and sober at the same time.'

Walsh pulled nervously at his flabby cheek. 'We ought to get away from this place. There's no telling what those devils may do now that King is dead. They're not civilized.'

'Who is, Mr Walsh, when it comes to the pinch?'

'We ought to get away.'

'I agree. But where to? Into the jungle?'

'It might be better than staying here.'

Helen Tudor was on her feet again and swaying to the rhythm of the tune. Barlow could imagine the microphone in front of her. Perhaps she was imagining it too, imagining the firelight to be the subdued lighting of a night club, those men just at the limits of her vision dinner-jacketed patrons who would clap her when the song was finished.

Fryer left his seat and staggered towards her. He put his right arm round her shoulders and drew her close to him.

Walsh again put a hand on Barlow's arm. 'You can't do anything. She asked for it. She won't take any harm.'

Barlow saw Fryer lose his balance and fall to the ground, dragging the woman with him. He still had his right arm round her and she was not trying to get away. Barlow heard her laugh.

'Come away,' Walsh said.

Barlow turned and walked at Walsh's side to the caves.

Katherine Summers and Evelyn Partridge were standing there looking towards the fire.

'You'd better go inside,' Barlow said.

Katherine asked: 'What are they doing over there?'

'They're drinking. Before long they'll all be dead drunk.'

'They're animals,' Mis Partridge said.

'We're all animals.'

'It's disgusting. And that woman. Drinking with them, dancing, singing. You'd think with poor Mr King just dead she'd have more sense of decency. And Mr Meade too. I thought she was in love with him. She forgets very easily.'

233

'Perhaps she doesn't,' Barlow said. 'Perhaps that's why she's over there.'

'I don't understand what you mean.'

'It doesn't matter. Will you go into the cave? It might be safer.'

'Surely you don't think they would assault us?'

'I don't know what they'll do. They may do anything. But given time they'll go to sleep.'

He himself went to the cave that had been King's, groped about in the darkness and found the boat-hook. He carried it out and sat down at the entrance to the women's cave. Walsh sat down beside him; he seemed to feel the need for company.

'They're dancing now,' Walsh said. 'Like a lot of dervishes.'

The fire was about eighty yards away from where they were sitting and they could see the figures of the men capering in the crimson glare, appearing and disappearing as the flames wavered. Now and then one of them would throw on more fuel and a fountain of sparks would spurt up into the night, dying almost

234

immediately. They could hear the shrill laughter of the woman.

'She's mad,' Walsh said.

'It's something that happens to people here. I'm sorry for her. She had a tough break.'

It was ten minutes later when they saw Lynch coming, treading a zigzag course towards the caves. Barlow stood up and waited for him, the boat-hook ready in his hands.

Lynch was chuckling to himself as if he had a joke that he was sharing with no one. The other three men had stayed by the fire, and the sound of their singing voices floated across from them. It was possible that they had not even noticed the disappearance of one of their number.

Lynch was close now. Barlow said suddenly: 'Where are you going?'

Lynch stopped, his head thrust forward, trying to make out Barlow's shape where he stood at the entrance to the women's cave.

'That you, bose? Thought you'd gone to sleep.'

'I'm not sleeping,' Barlow said. 'What do you want?'

Lynch chuckled again. 'What you think I want? A woman, that's what. Not the old bitch neither. The young one.'

'Go back where you came from. Get yourself another drink and forget it.'

'I don't want another drink. Not right now. Later maybe. Right now I want the woman.'

'You're drunk,' Barlow said. 'Get to hell out of it.'

'I ain't getting out. I may be drunk, but not too drunk. I'm going in, see. And you ain't stopping me neither.'

He came closer to Barlow, breathing fumes of rum over the bosun. He was a scarecrow of a man, the clothes hanging limply on his bony frame; but he could be a dangerous scarecrow.

'I'm warning you,' Barlow said.

Lynch spat on the ground. 'You warning me. You better get things straight, bose. There's a new order here. From now on it's share and share alike. No more favourites. Now are you getting out of my way?'

Barlow laid his hand flat on Lynch's chest and pushed. 'Go back to your pals, Sammy.'

Lynch staggered but did not fall. For a man who had drunk so much his reflexes were in surprisingly good order.

Walsh shouted a warning: 'He's got a knife.'

Barlow had also seen the knife. He made a swift, sideways lunge with the boat-hook and heard the thud as it made contact with Lynch's head. Lynch went down without even a cry.

Walsh peered down at the crumpled heap. 'Do you think he's badly hurt?'

'Not badly enough,' Barlow said. 'When he wakes up he may have changed his ideas. He'll have a hangover anyway. I wouldn't want his hangover. No, sir.'

17

Morning After

Barlow went down to the beach at the first sign of light. He went past the ashes of the fire and saw the men lying on the ground and sleeping off their drunkenness.

Grimes lay with his head close to the cask, as though he were protecting the precious liquid from robbery. Peering inside, Barlow saw that it was still more than two-thirds full; there was plenty for another debauch, but at this rate of consumption it would not last long.

The idea came into his mind that now, with the others asleep, it might be advisable to empty the cask of its remaining contents; in that way he would make sure that there would be no repetition of the previous night's revelry. But he decided against the plan. Fryer and Grimes would guess at once who had robbed them of their liquor, and then there would be trouble. These men were as dangerous sober as drunk, perhaps even more dangerous. There was no point in goading them unnecessarily.

The light was coming rapidly, but inland there was still darkness. It was into that darkness that he would have to plunge again if any of them were to escape — he and Walsh and the women. It would be a hard journey for all of them, but it was one that would have to be faced.

He saw Fryer lying on his back and snoring. He stooped over the big man, searching for the revolver, the seal of authority, but it was not in Fryer's belt. They had been too cunning for that; they had hidden the weapon before they had gone to sleep. He suspected here the work of Grimes. Fryer would have been too far gone to think of it, but Grimes had had his wits about him, rum or no rum, and the revolver was not there.

Helen Tudor was not there either. He wondered where she had gone, but he was not greatly worried about her; she was a woman who had had a lot of experience and could look after herself. Yet even the hard-boiled ones had their soft spots, and Helen Tudor's soft spot had been Arnold Meade. She had been hit badly by his death, no doubt about that.

He stirred the ashes and saw that there was still a glow at the centre of the fire. He left it and continued on his way to the beach.

She was lying where the tide had left her like a piece of jetsam. She was naked, lying face downward with her arms stretched out and her hair like a golden weed scattered in a fan about her head and shoulders. The scum from the retreating tide lay along her body in a white border, marking out the exact extent of her claim upon the beach. There was a shallow depression where she lay; it had taken the shape of her figure, so that when Barlow bent down and lifted her in his arms there was left the perfect mould of a woman in the sand.

Barlow carried her to the place where the men were sleeping. Her face looked older now and her skin was cold; it was cold under his fingers and cold on his bare chest. He stood there by the ashes of the dead fire, holding her in his arms, and he kicked Fryer until the seaman woke and stared up at him with bleary eyes.

'Who's that? What you want?'

'It's me — Barlow. I've got a present for you.'

'A present! What you blabbing about? What you got there?'

'The woman,' Barlow said.

Fryer was fully awake now. He lifted himself on one elbow, winced as he felt a stab of pain in his bandaged hand, and licked scummy lips.

'What you doing with her? She's my woman now. You leave her alone. She's mine, see?'

'She's no use to you, Ben; no use at all.'

'What do you mean, no use?'

'She's dead,' Barlow said.

Fryer tried to shake the last traces of sleep out of his brain. He stared at Barlow, accusation in his dull eyes. 'You killed her. You'll pay for this. What you want to kill her for?'

Barlow said coldly: 'I didn't kill her. She was drowned. Maybe she drowned herself. I don't know. Makes no difference

241

anyway. She's dead. And if anybody killed her, you did.'

He left Fryer and walked away with the body of Helen Tudor. There would be another burial, another depletion of the strength of the colony. There were only eight now. Eight little nigger boys.

And four of them had better get away before the number dropped still lower. They would have to make their plans and carry them out quickly.

★ ★ ★

The drunks woke one by one as the sun began to scorch them. Lynch had a bruise on the side of his head where the boat-hook had struck him. His memory of the incident was hazy, but he seemed to remember something of an encounter with Barlow. When he saw Barlow he said: 'Did you hit me last night?'

'Why should I hit you?' Barlow asked.

Lynch touched the bruise. 'See this? Where'd I get this if you didn't hit me?'

'Maybe you ran into something. You were drunk enough.'

'Maybe I did and maybe I didn't. But there's some here need to watch their step. I'm telling you.'

'And I'm listening,' Barlow said. 'I'll remember it.'

Lynch went away with his ragged trousers flapping loosely.

'There's one with a sore head,' Walsh said.

'He's not the only one. There'll be some vicious tempers until they get themselves drunk again.'

'When will that be?'

'I don't know. They may save it for the evening.'

'What do you think they'll do then? With Helen dead.'

'It doesn't take much working out. Tonight Lynch may not come alone.'

'That's what I was thinking.'

'We'd better get ready,' Barlow said. 'This looks to me like moving day.'

★ ★ ★

They had to make their preparations secretly. They would need to carry as

243

much food and water as possible. There were two blankets that had been salvaged from the boat and they decided to take these also.

Barlow told the two women of their plans. 'We shall have to get away as soon as we can after nightfall. They'll have started drinking again by then. With any luck they won't notice that we've gone until we're well on our way.'

'I suppose it is essential to go?' Miss Partridge said. 'It will be a difficult journey and we don't know where it will lead.'

'It isn't safe here any longer. You know what happened last night. It will get worse.'

'I think we should go,' Katherine said. 'I won't feel safe until we're away from this place.'

The death of Helen Tudor had been a shock to her, more of a shock than any of the other deaths. Walsh had suggested that it might have been an accident, that in her drunken state she had fallen on the beach and the tide had come up over her. In his own mind Barlow had no doubt that the singer had drowned herself, but he did not voice this opinion.

★　★　★

It was a day of tension. Suspicion was in the air. Fryer watched Barlow with bloodshot eyes and fingered the butt of the revolver which had returned to his belt. Lynch watched him also, his expression venomous. McKay slept and Grimes moved about from one place to another, watching everyone, missing nothing. It was Grimes whom Barlow feared more than Fryer. Fryer was an obtuse, leaden-brained man, but Grimes was nimble-witted and not so easy to hoodwink.

The hours passed slowly. Barlow thought of going for a last swim but decided against it. Walsh was restless and nervous, and it was he whom Fryer chose to taunt.

'Hey, you — passenger — plutocrat — whatever you call yourself.'

Fryer was lying in the shade of one of the palm trees, his back resting against the bole, his shirt open to reveal the barrel chest and part of his stomach.

'Come here, you financial wizard.'

Walsh approached Fryer hesitantly. 'Were you addressing me?'

Fryer mimicked him. 'Was I addressing him! Who in hell do you think I was addressing?' He rubbed his lips with a a stubby finger. 'I want a talk with you Mr Stephen Walsh.'

Walsh coughed nervously, watching Fryer with apprehension. 'I can't think what you would wish to talk to me about, Mr Fryer.'

'You can't, can't you? Well, how about the subject of money for a start?'

'Money?'

'That's it. You heard of the stuff, ain't you? What you spend. What rich men like you have a lot of.'

'I'm not a rich man.'

Fryer laughed derisively, and Lynch and McKay joined in.

'Not a rich man? Don't give me that. If you wasn't rich you wouldn't be taking a trip round the world.'

'It was doctor's orders. I was told to

take a long voyage for the sake of my health.'

The three seamen laughed again. 'So it was for your health,' Fryer said. 'Well, it's done your health some good, I must say. You're in first-class condition now.'

'I'm a sick man,' Walsh said.

'You ain't sick,' Fryer said. 'You're just a lazy bastard with too much money. I bet you never done any real hard graft in your life.'

'We can't all do manual labour.' Walsh sounded apologetic about it. 'Some of us have to do the brain-work.'

Fryer spat. 'So you're one of the brainy ones. I reckon you think you're a sight too clever for me.'

'I didn't say that.'

'But it's what you meant. Mr Walsh, I can read your mind like it was a Sunday newspaper. I know what you're thinking. You're thinking here's this poor stupid bastard of a seaman what's bone from the neck up and here's me with my first class brain. I'm superior to him. Be rights I shouldn't even be lowering meself to talk to him. I'm superior to all these horrible

247

coarse seamen. I despise them.'

'I don't despise you,' Walsh said. He wanted to get away. He did not like the trend of this conversation. He knew that Fryer was working up a grievance and it scared him. He ought to walk away, but he knew that if he did so Fryer might fly into a rage. Therefore he stayed where he was, tugging nervously at the cord of his disreputable dressing-gown.

Fryer sneered. 'So you don't despise me. Well, that's nice to know. That's almighty civil of you. But maybe that's because I ain't important enough to be despised. You don't despise dirt, do you? You don't even think about it.'

Walsh began to edge away. Perhaps if he moved slowly Fryer would not notice that he was going. Perhaps Fryer would lose interest in him. But he was wrong.

'Come back, Walsh,' Fryer said.

'I have to go. I've got things to do.'

'You ain't got nothing to do, not unless I tell you to. Come here. Come close where I can see you proper.'

Walsh reluctantly obeyed.

'I got something for you to do,' Fryer

said. 'A job I been wanting to give one of you upper class swine for years.'

'What sort of job?' Walsh asked.

'A nice easy job. It'll suit you. Lick my feet.'

Walsh stared down at Fryer's feet. They were bare, deformed, the toe-nails broken and dirty. He instinctively recoiled and Fryer swore at him.

'Go on. Get down on your knees and do it.'

Lynch and McKay were grinning, delighting in the humilation of a man like Walsh, a man who wore a silk dressing-gown.

'That's the idea, Ben,' Lynch said. 'It's us what've been licking the boots of his sort for long enough. Now it's his turn.'

Walsh said pleadingly: 'You can't mean that. You're joking.'

'The joke's on you then. Get down and do it.'

'I won't do it,' Walsh said, but he spoke without conviction. 'I refuse.'

Fryer reacted quickly. He dragged the revolver out of his belt and levelled it at Walsh's stomach.

'So you'd rather have a slug in the guts.'

Walsh looked at the revolver and had no doubt in his mind that Fryer would not hesitate to shoot. Cut off from the restraints of civilization, these men had degenerated rapidly; they had become dangerous animals, savage beasts with little concern for the sanctity of human life. And Fryer was the worst of them. Walsh believed that Fryer would have been prepared to shoot a man in the stomach just for the devilment of it.

'Put the gun away,' he said. 'I'll do it.'

He went down on his knees and began to lick Fryer's feet. Fryer put the revolver back in his belt and laughed. Lynch and McKay laughed also. Walsh felt the humiliation of it like a sickness inside him. He knew that Barlow would not have done it; Barlow would not have so degraded himself even to save his own life.

Fryer dismissed him at last with a kick in the mouth. Walsh could taste blood on his tongue, but it was better than the other taste.

'Now get away with you,' Fryer said. 'You make me sick.'

250

Walsh got up from his knees and went to wash his mouth out. He could hear the men laughing.

* * *

Grimes was keeping an eye on Barlow. Grimes was suspicious. He was a man who trusted no one; it was doubtful whether he even trusted himself.

'You ain't thinking up some plan, are you, bose? Something you wouldn't be confiding to a pal.'

'Who's the pal?' Barlow asked.

'Why, me, bose. Yours very truly. You wouldn't be cooking up some scheme what I didn't have no part of, would you? Likewise what Ben and Andy and Sammy didn't have no part of.'

'What sort of scheme would that be, pally?'

'Like a scheme for getting away from here. Like a scheme for four people going off and leaving the other four behind.'

'I don't know why you should think anything like that. Why would anyone

251

want to get away from this earthly paradise?'

Grimes's mouth twisted in a contortion that might have been a smile. 'Paradise is right. So don't try nothing, bose. It wouldn't work. I reckon the only way out is the way Meade took, and you don't want to go that way, do you?'

'No,' Barlow said. 'I don't.'

'Then watch it.'

'I will.'

He watched Grimes moving away with his queer, gliding walk that reminded you somehow of a shadow slipping lightly and silently over the ground.

'Damn him,' Barlow muttered. 'Damn the filthy little runt. I'd like to break his stinking neck.'

18

Flight

With the coming of darkness the fire was rekindled and the serious rum drinking began again.

Barlow and Walsh stood by the cliff and watched the other men in the firelight.

'Do we go now?' Walsh asked.

'Wait a little,' Barlow said. 'The drunker they are, the less fit they'll be to follow us.'

'Suppose they come for the women.'

'We'll keep an eye on them. If anyone comes this way we'll move out fast.'

'I think we ought to go now.'

'We have to pass too close to the fire. Let them get drunk first.'

They could see a figure doling out the rum. It could have been Grimes, but at such a distance it was impossible to be certain. They heard a sudden shout of laughter.

Overhead the stars were visible, but

away in the distance a black mountain of cloud had blotted them out. A flicker of lightning traced a path across the cloud and was followed by a low rumble of thunder.

'There's a nasty storm over there,' Walsh said uneasily. 'Let's hope it doesn't come this way.'

'It could be a help.'

The two women came out of the cave and stood with Barlow and Walsh, watching the fire.

'Everything is ready,' Miss Partridge said. 'When do we start?'

'Soon,' Barlow said.

'Do you think we can get to the top of the mountain tonight?'

'No, I don't think that's possible, not in the dark. It would be too dangerous. We'll try to reach the waterfall and stay there until daybreak. Then we'll go on.'

'You think they'll follow us?'

'Perhaps. But if they drink as much rum as they did last night they won't be in any condition to make a chase of it. We should be able to shake them off.'

Half an hour later Barlow said: 'All

right. Let's be on our way.'

They loaded themselves with the provisions they had collected, Barlow and Walsh carrying the rolled blankets. Barlow took the boat-hook and they moved silently along the foot of cliff, making for the cover of the trees.

The firelight flickered on the cliff as the flames leaped in the breeze that had sprung up and they felt exposed. But the men by the fire gave no sign of having seen them. They were singing now, and the sound of their voices came discordantly across the intervening stretch of ground.

'Animals,' Miss Partridge said softly. She was following Katherine, who was just behind Barlow. Walsh brought up the rear, a weird-looking figure in his ragged dressing-gown and dirty pyjamas.

'Animals,' Miss Partridge said again, setting her feet carefully on the rough ground. She heard Walsh stumble and mutter something, and she glanced over her shoulder at the dark figure close behind her. 'Are you all right, Mr Walsh?'

'I stubbed my toe.'

Walsh was feeling sick. There was a fluttering sensation in the pit of his stomach. He had told Fryer the truth when he had said that he was a sick man; he was doubtful whether anyone as sick as he was could hope to survive a journey through the jungle if it was as bad as Barlow had said it was. Yet to stay here was unthinkable.

Miss Partridge stopped suddenly and he bumped into her.

'Sorry,' he mumbled. 'Didn't see — '

Then he heard Grimes's voice coming from the darkness just ahead. He could not see Grimes but the voice was unmistakeable.

'So you didn't take my advice, bose. You thought you'd be too clever for me.'

Walsh tried to peer round Miss Partridge. He could just make out the vague shapes of Katherine and Barlow and a smaller figure that must be Grimes.

'Not so clever really though,' Grimes went on. 'Me and my mates, we thought something like this might happen and we was prepared. You don't think we go about with our eyes shut, do you? We got brains.

256

Maybe you thought all the brains was on your side. But no, Mr Barlow, not so.'

'Get out of the way, Bart,' Barlow said. 'We're coming past.'

'Not past, bose. Back. Back where you come from. All of you. Specially the ladies. We got a party laid on for the female section. Wouldn't be much of a do without them.'

'Get out of the way,' Barlow said again. 'We're not going back. If you try to stop us it'll just be too bad for you.'

Grimes laughed derisively. 'You don't scare me, bose. I only got to shout. Why don't you be sensible?'

There was a flicker of lightning, brighter than any of the previous flashes. It revealed Grimes clearly for a moment and then was gone, leaving a thicker darkness.

'No night for travelling,' Grimes said. 'You going to be sensible?'

Barlow took a step forward. 'I warned you, Bart.' He swung the boat-hook, but Grimes was not there. The boat-hook slashed the air and met no resistance.

Grimes began to yell at the top of his

voice: 'This way, Ben. Over here. They're making a break. Over here.'

Barlow swung at him again, felt the boat-hook strike home and heard Grimes cursing.

Katherine cried in alarm: 'His knife, Chris! Look out for his knife!'

It was the knife that had killed King. Barlow swayed to one side and felt the blade slide across his left forearm, the razorsharp edge biting into the flesh.

He held the boat-hook close and swung it in a short downward arc. He heard the thud as it struck Grimes's head, and the man went down and the knife slipped from his hand. Barlow picked it up and gave it to the girl.

'Hang on to his. It might be useful. Now all of you, quick, after me.'

He did not need to urge them. They could hear Fryer and Lynch and McKay coming. And Fryer had the gun.

Barlow led them on a slanting course towards the trees where they would be able to merge into the shadows, becoming shadows themselves.

Walsh's legs were trembling; they felt

like jelly. He tripped and fell; he tried to get up and his legs refused to obey the commands of his brain. Now he knew that the others would leave him; he would be left to the mercy of Ben Fryer, that man who had made him lick his feet. In his weakness he wanted to cry like a lost child.

Then he heard Barlow's voice, savage now. 'Get up, damn you.' Barlow's hand was under his armpit and Evelyn Partridge was on the other side, lifting him.

'Leave me,' he whimpered. 'I can't walk.' But he did not want them to leave him. He was afraid.

'You can walk,' Miss Partridge said. 'You can run.'

He found that he could. He found that when they had helped him to his feet he was able to run with them. He wondered why the seamen had not overtaken them; he seemed to have been lying on the ground for so long. He did not realize that it had been only a few seconds.

He ran with his pounding heart and his legs of jelly, the dressing-gown flapping about his knees like a shroud. He ran with the blood throbbing in his ears, with his throat like sandpaper and a pain stabbing at his side. I can't go on, he thought; I can't go any further. I shall drop down dead. I can't go on.

And he went on.

'Stop now,' Barlow said.

They stopped, and the sound of their breathing was like another breeze. The trees were round them, hiding them. Somewhere in the distance a man was shouting. Another answered him.

Barlow said: 'We've given them the slip — for the moment. We'll get our wind, then we'll press on.'

'I'm done for,' Walsh said. The jelly in his legs gave way again and he sat down suddenly. 'I've had all I can take.'

'You'll take some more,' Barlow said pitilessly.

And Miss Partridge added: 'Don't give in, Mr Walsh. You can't give in now.'

He felt her hand touching his cheek; it was cool and gentle. He felt stronger simply from the touch of it, as though some of her strength had flowed into his body through the contact of those fingers.

'You will go on, won't you?'

'Yes,' he said. 'I will go on.'

The rain began to fall as they started again, and it was so dark that Barlow ordered each one of them to keep a hand on the one immediately ahead to prevent any possibility of their becoming separated. He himself led the way, moving partly by instinct and partly by the intermittent illumination of the lightning.

Almost at once they were drenched to the skin. The water ran from them in streams and the soil under their feet was turned to squelching mud. The wind became stronger, whipping the trees into a mad dance that was revealed one moment and hidden the next as the lightning produced a vivid alternation of day and night.

They came out of the trees at last and saw the waterfall like a ribbon of silver dropping from the sky. The lightning flashed upon it and was reflected in a thousand splinters of light, while the rain still fell in a ceaseless torrent.

'We shall have to find some shelter,'

Barlow shouted. He remembered a rock that he had seen on his previous expedition jutting out over a natural cavity. Perhaps if he could find that rock it would provide some protection from the weather.

'Stay here,' he said. 'I'm going to look.'

He found the rock without difficulty and led the others to it. There was room beneath for all of them. They were drenched and shivering, but they huddled together and drew what comfort they could from contact with one another.

Until this moment Barlow had given scarcely a thought to the cut in his left arm. Now he could feel it throbbing.

At the same instant Katherine asked: 'How is your arm. That man cut it, didn't he?'

'It's not too bad,' Barlow said. 'I'll tie a handkerchief round it.'

He pulled the handkerchief from his pocket and suddenly felt the girl's fingers in the darkness helping to tie it.

'Thank you,' he said. 'You're a good girl, Katie.'

Walsh was breathing heavily, wheezing

like a sufferer from asthma. He sounded plaintive.

'We chose a fine night to start travelling.'

'It's probably the best sort of night we could have,' Barlow said. 'I don't think the others will come far in this.'

'You think we're safe here?' Evelyn Partridge asked.

'We shan't be safe until we're in the jungle on the other side of the mountain.'

'But we're not as far as that yet,' Walsh said and began to shiver again.

* * *

It was Katherine who saw Fryer first. He was standing by the pool at the foot of the waterfall and a flash of lightning revealed him unmistakably, his smooth brown head shining with moisture, his long arms hanging loosely like a gorilla's.

'There's Fryer.'

They all saw him when the next flash came. He had turned and was staring towards the rock. They could see the revolver in his belt.

'He's seen us,' Walsh muttered.

'No,' Barlow said. 'He couldn't see in here. But he's suspicious. He may come to look. I'm going out.'

He felt the girl's hand. 'You can't do that. He might kill you.'

'He won't kill me. I'll see to that. But if we all stay here he's bound to find us. I'll head him off.'

He slipped out from the cover of the rock into the darkness outside. When the next flash revealed the stark outline of the trees he was thirty yards away. He saw Fryer swing round and knew that the man had seen him.

Fryer gave a yell and began to run towards him, tugging at the revolver. Then it was dark again and Barlow went into the darkness, moving across the lower slopes of the mountain and glancing back whenever the lightning came to make certain that Fryer was still following. He had to keep Fryer at a respectable distance because of the revolver, but it was essential that he should not shake the man off altogether. He had to draw him away from the rock where the others were hidden; it was the manoeuvre of the mother bird that draws the marauder away from the nest of young ones.

They were in among the trees again now, the ground squelching under their feet and creepers lying across the way to trip the unwary. Suddenly Barlow heard Fryer's bellow, audible even above the other noises.

'Stop there! Stop or I'll plug you.'

Barlow ran on. He had left the boat-hook under the rock and he was carrying nothing. He felt fresh and strong, able to outrun and outwit Fryer with ease. It was almost too simple.

But when the next flicker of lightning came he looked back and could not see Fryer; there was no pursuer stumbling along behind him. He had gone too quickly and had dropped the man sooner than he had intended. He came to a halt and rested one hand against a tree, gazing back into the darkness. Lightning illuminated the scene again but revealed no sign of Fryer.

He shouted: 'Where are you, Ben? Have

you lost me? Here I am. Come and get me.'

The lightning snaked down and almost in the same instant he heard the crack of the revolver. He heard a bullet imbed itself in the trunk close to his hand and he caught a glimpse of Fryer away to the right before blackness clamped down again.

He had under-estimated Fryer. The man was not such a fool, not so easy after all. The revolver stabbed again out of the darkness, but Fryer was firing blindly this time and the bullet went wide.

Barlow let out a scream of pain and then moved quickly and silently away from the spot where he had been standing. He heard Fryer approaching, making no attempt at silence, eager to finish what he believed the last shot had begun.

Barlow waited for him, but not at the place where Fryer was expecting him to be. Fryer reached the spot where the body should have been lying and found nothing.

Barlow could hear him muttering to

himself: 'The sly bastard. He had me there. He wasn't hit. Or maybe he was at that; maybe it was just a little hit. Well, I'll get him now. I'll get him.'

There was no sound of Fryer's moving. Barlow guessed that he was standing still, listening. Barlow also stood still, not making a sound.

Eventually Fryer became tired of waiting. He moved away from the tree, and at that moment lightning slashed down through the branches. Barlow leaped at Fryer and locked his right arm round Fryer's neck. Fryer reacted violently; he braced his muscles and swayed from side to side in an attempt to dislodge his attacker. But Barlow tightened his grip and Fryer began to choke. The revolver was still in his hand but he was not in a position to use it effectively. He fired one shot and then dropped the weapon in the mud. He clawed at Barlow's arm, trying desperately to loose it from his throat, but he was becoming weaker and strength was slipping away from his fingers. Barlow's arm remained clamped about his neck like the thick coil of a boa constrictor, immovable.

When Barlow felt the weight of Fryer on his arm he knew that the brief struggle was finished. He let Fryer drop to the ground and stood there for a while panting from the exertion.

Then he began to search for the revolver, but could not find it. He groped about in the mud while a continuous cascade of water poured down from the branches of the trees. It was a world of water, a world of slime and rottenness, where everything that he touched seemed to disintegrate beneath his fingers.

He abandoned the search at last and, leaving Fryer where he lay, made his way back to the others.

19

The Clever One

Before morning the storm had passed and the sky was cloudless. The sun came up and lifted the water from the ground in an ascending column of steam. Climbing the mountain was a sweaty exercise in the atmosphere of a Turkish bath and their clothes clung to their bodies with the damp clasp of saturation. There was a stiffness in their limbs from the cramped cell in which they had spent the night, but this passed off as they climbed, as the sun shone upon them and the warmth spread through their bones.

Again, inevitably, it was Walsh who lagged, who found the going hard. His ridiculous clothing hampered him, the dressing-gown catching on bushes and crags and winding itself about his legs in a way that threatened to trip him and send him rolling down the slope. It was only

Barlow's constant goading that kept him from giving up completely.

'Come on, damn you. Come on,' Barlow snarled.

Walsh was shaking. He wondered whether he had a fever; malaria perhaps. His head was swimming; the sun dazzled him. Above him the mountain stretched away, apparently limitless. He was an insect crawling up the wall of a sky-scraper; it was impossible, a task utterly beyond his powers.

'I can't go any further. I'm exhausted.'

'You're not exhausted. You're just a fat, lazy slob.' Barlow stood above him, looking down in accusation.

'Leave me alone,' Walsh said hopelessly. 'I've had enough.' He could feel the sweat trickling down the back of his neck. He felt sick and weak.

'You're coming with us,' Barlow said. 'You're coming with us if I have to drag you to the top by your ears.' He reached down towards Walsh with the boat-hook. 'Grab hold of that. Grab it, do you hear? Get your damned fingers round it.'

Walsh heard. He gripped the boat-hook

in both hands and allowed himself to be helped up.

They went on.

★　★　★

The sun was high when they reached the summit. It glowered down upon the three idols like a brazen eye. The wind moaned in their hollow bellies and they were as they had been when Barlow had first seen them, unchanged, unchangeable until the timber should become rotten, until decay should attack their stiff bodies, turning them to dust.

There they stood, grinning, with their great gaping mouths and staring eyes, products of man's need for something to worship, his longing for a god, even if that god should be nothing but a hideous caricature of himself carved by himself from the lifeless wood of a felled tree.

'How perfectly horrible,' Katherine said, shuddering.

They stood in a compact group, staring at the idols, a gap of thirty yards lying between themselves and those monstrous figures rising from the flat top of the mountain like the last remaining pillars of a ruined temple. The idols towered over them, moaning and whistling as though it were agony to stand there rooted in the ground, unable to retreat from the fierce heat of the sun or find shelter from any storm that might come sweeping its trail of desolation along the ridge.

'So these are your idols,' Walsh said. He was feeling better now that the climb had been completed. He even felt a little ashamed of the weakness he had shown in front of the women and he wanted to talk away the memory. 'They are certainly not remarkable for their beauty. Can't say I care for their singing either.'

Miss Partridge was amazed by the size of them. 'How were they dragged up here? It must have been a colossal task.'

'You can do anything if you have enough hands,' Barlow said. 'I suppose there was no lack of man-power.'

'Then where has it gone now? We have seen no one.'

'Perhaps they moved on. Perhaps they all died. I have seen skeletons.'

He moved forward, the boat-hook trailing in his right hand, and as he did so Grimes stepped out from behind the middle idol.

'You took your time getting here,' Grimes said. He had the revolver in his right hand and there was a dirty bandage tied round his head. He was grinning, but there was nothing pleasant about the grin; it was venomous; and there was venom in his speech also. 'I been waiting. You didn't oughter keep a gentleman waiting. Not polite.'

Barlow had stopped. He rested the end of the boat-hook on the ground and looked at Grimes. 'It seems I didn't hit you hard enough. A pity.'

'You hit me hard enough all right,' Grimes said. 'You hit me a sight too hard for your own good. You better drop the boat-hook.'

Barlow hesitated and Grimes snarled at him viciously: 'I said drop it.' He jerked the revolver. 'I ain't taking any funny business. You better get that into your big head straight off. Drop it.'

Barlow opened his hand and the

boat-hook clattered to the ground. Grimes nodded.

'That's the style. Obey orders like a good boy. I'm giving 'em now. I'm the new boss.'

'How did you get the gun?'

'How did I get it? Why Ben give it to me. You treated him rough, you did. Near croaked him, so he says. Got a sore neck has our Ben and ain't feeling so good, so he lent me the gun. Maybe he'll get it back, maybe he won't. This little bit of ironmongery's a handy thing to have around the place. Makes you twice as tall, twice as big.'

'So you're feeling big now?'

'Pretty big, mate, pretty big.'

Barlow was wondering how Fryer had managed to find the revolver when he regained consciousness. He was angry with himself for having missed it. It had been there all the time; he ought to have made a better search.

Grimes seemed to read his thoughts. 'You'd be in a different spot now if you'd got the gun, wouldn't you? Maybe you hunted for it; but you couldn't find it, could you? And for why? Because it was hid, that's why?'

'Hidden? Where?'

'Under old Ben. He told me it was sticking into his guts when he woke up. Lucky it didn't go off and blow a hole in him. Lucky for him, lucky for me, not so flamin' lucky for you.'

Walsh said: 'How did you get here? How did you know?'

Grimes looked at him, head on one side, the dirty bandage like a truncated turban. 'How did I know you would be coming this way? It was simple. This was the way the bosun came first time, wasn't it? That's what he told us. Stands to reason he'd come this way again. So I got here early by another route and then I waited. I'm the clever one, I am.'

'What are you going to do? What's the game?'

Grimes lowered the revolver and scratched his stomach with his left hand, but his beady eyes were alert and watchful. He let his gaze linger for a while on Katherine Summers with anticipatory pleasure.

'What am I going to do, hey? That's an easy question to answer. I'm going to take you back. The fact is we've got so much attached to you, me and my mates, that we can't bear to lose the blessing of your company. Made our hearts fair bleed to think you were aiming to get away and leave us.'

'Made your head bleed too,' Barlow said.

The twist of Grimes's mouth was venomous again. 'Maybe we'll settle that score later. I ain't forgotten. There's some things what have to be paid for. We'll talk about that when we get back to the beach.'

'Suppose we don't want to go back to the beach. Suppose we say we're going in the opposite direction.'

'Well, then,' Grimes said, 'it would have to be a case of persuasion, wouldn't it?' He lifted the revolver a little way and let it fall again to his side. 'This here's a great persuader.' He glanced again at Katherine Summers and added thoughtfully: 'Of course we could come to another arrangement.'

'What would that be?'

'Suppose two of you was to go down there.' Grimes pointed towards the jungle. 'And suppose the other two was to come back with me.'

'Which two?'

'Well, it wouldn't hardly be right for the ladies to go on a long journey through that there jungle, would it? Nasty things in there, so I'm told. Let's say then that Mr Walsh and you go off on your ownsome and good luck to you. And let's say I escort the female section back to the fo'c'sle like.'

'Go back to your mates,' Barlow said. 'You're wasting your time here. If you know what's good for you, you'll get moving straightaway.'

'I know what's good for me,' Grimes snarled. 'And I mean to have it.'

'No,' Barlow said.

Grimes lifted the revolver until the muzzle was again pointing at Barlow's stomach. 'It wouldn't pain me none to let you have it, bose. Are you going to see sense?'

'No.'

Grimes pulled back the hammer of the revolver with his thumb, but Barlow was not looking at the gun; he was looking at the snake.

The snake came from the mouth of the tallest idol. It was long and thin as a stock-whip. It came out smoothly, its head waving from side to side, its tongue darting in and out. Its eyes were like dark ice.

Barlow said: 'Look behind you, Bart. There's a snake.'

Grimes laughed derisively. 'You think I was born yesterday? You think I'm the boy to be taken in by that gag? I'm the clever one. I told you.'

'Maybe not as clever as you think.' Barlow was watching the snake; it had begun to slither down the trunk of the idol, but its tail was still in the mouth. It looked like a long thin tongue. 'Not if you get a bite from that joker.'

'I told you it won't work,' Grimes said, but a shade of doubt had crept into his voice. The others were all looking beyond him, into the emptiness behind his back. If it was empty.

'You don't scare me,' he said.

Walsh's hands were plucking nervously at his dressing-gown. 'There is a snake. There is.'

The sound that the snake made as it touched the ground was a small sound, but Grimes had keen hearing and was on the alert. He heard the sound and knew that there was something behind him. He swung round and saw the snake. The snake lifted its head and hissed.

Grimes fired one shot with the revolver and then another. The bullets scattered dust from the ground and a few splinters of rock, but they did not hit the snake.

Grimes was about to fire a third time when Barlow crashed into him. He staggered under the impact and Barlow got a grip on the hand that was holding the revolver. The third shot sang away into the air as Barlow jerked Grimes's arm back until the bones crunched.

Grimes struggled viciously. He kicked back at Barlow's shins and lunged suddenly forward, taking the bosun with him. Locked together they staggered a few yards and then, unable to keep their balance, fell heavily to the ground.

The snake, frightened by the shots, had started to wriggle away, but it was too late; the two men, with Grimes underneath, fell upon it as it squirmed through the dust. In their own struggle they had forgotten the deadly reptile.

The snake reacted like a coiled spring suddenly released. Its head whipped upward and the fangs sank into the flesh of Grimes's neck.

Grimes began to scream.

20

Transport

The dark world had closed upon them; the dark, hot, humid world of trees and creepers, of fronds and undergrowth, of clinging mud, of leeches, of a million biting insects and the chattering, shrieking, disembodied voices that howled at them night and day. And here, waiting for Barlow, was the ghost of Lanyon with his mud-stopped jaws, lurking behind every tree, in every patch of shadow.

'Where are we heading?' Walsh asked.

'We have to reach the river,' Barlow said. 'That's our first objective. The river.'

But he could not find the river. As they moved forward the river receded. Was it a dream that he had dreamed? Had there never been a river? Had there been no dead village, no skeletons? Had he perhaps murdered Lanyon and fled from the jungle? Was that the way it had been?

'We have been travelling for six days,' Walsh said. 'You said it was only two or three days' journey to the river.'

Walsh was a distressing sight; he was haggard and mudstained; the dressing-gown and pyjamas hung on him in tatters. He had sustained a cut in his left leg and the leg had begun to swell; it felt stiff and unatural, like a wooden limb that had been fastened on to him when he was not looking. It frightened him.

'If it was true what you said, we should have reached it by now. Perhaps there isn't a river.'

'If we didn't have to travel so slowly because of you,' Barlow said, 'we should have got to it days ago. The river is there.'

But he could not be certain in his own heart. Nothing was certain any more, nothing but the dripping trees, the oppressive heat and the stench of decay, nothing but the voices and the ghosts.

It was the women who remained strong and uncomplaining. Miss Partridge watched over Walsh as a mother might watch over her child. Perhaps it was some memory of a former existence in which she had been a ship's stewardess and he a passenger that pointed her to this duty. Or perhaps it was a feeling of pity, a desire as she saw him stumbling like a sick man to help him onward, to counteract his weakness with her strength.

Mostly he took all her attentions for granted, but there were times when he seemed to appreciate what she was doing.

'You are very good to me, Evelyn.'

Until then he had always called her Miss Partridge. She had not realized that he even knew her other name. But he used it now quite naturally, as though he had called her that always.

'About that nephew of yours; I'll do what I can when we get back.'

'My nephew?'

'You wanted me to give him a job. Don't you remember?'

'I had forgotten. It's not important.'

'But it is important. I shall see to it at once when we get back. I shall speak to Jackson. We can use good men.'

She knew that he was trying to convince himself that he would get back, that a time would really come when he would again be in a position to hand out jobs to deserving people. It was something to cling to, like a raft in a raging sea.

'I built up that business from the ground. Only a few hundred pounds of capital. I had to work. Fryer said I'd never worked, but I have. It wasn't all easy going, I can tell you.'

'I'm sure it wasn't.'

He was like a child boasting about the things he had done. There was indeed something pathetically childlike about Stephen Walsh as he sat there in his ragged dressing-gown, talking and talking in a vain attempt to bring the world of his success closer and thrust away this other world of disaster and degradation.

'It's still a private company. We've never gone public. Everything's come out of profits; never had to borrow a penny. Last year's turnover was a record.'

'You must have been pleased with that,' Miss Partridge said, wiping the mud from his face with a damp cloth. 'I never had any head for business. I'm sure I could never understand it. So complicated.'

'Well, yes, it is complicated,' Walsh

admitted with a certain complacency. 'Rather above a woman's head, I'd say. Of course we employ women, but you couldn't leave the running of the business to them; it'd be down the drain in no time.'

The thought of the business going down the drain brought Jackson into his mind and the worry of what reckless things Jackson might be doing. 'I should never have left it. Doctors — what do they know? Said I was suffering from overwork. Well, got to admit I had been pressing myself a bit hard, but nothing to worry about really. Should never have let them stampede me. Now look at the mess.'

'It will be all right in the end,' Miss Partridge said soothingly. 'We've just got to be patient.'

'Patient! Well, good God! Patient!' His nervous fingers plucked at the cord of the dressing-gown. 'I should think I've got as much patience as the next fellow, but there is a limit. Really, you know, it's too bad, too bad by half. If only I'd taken a different ship. Ships have no business to blow up, not in peace time. War's different; you expect it. But not in peace time. And then if only we'd been in a different boat. I expect all the others were picked up. It was that man King's fault. He ought to be punished.'

'He's dead,' Miss Partridge said.

'Dead! Yes, that's so.' Walsh appeared to have forgotten the fact until reminded of it. 'Dead. Well, he deserved it, didn't he? It was only justice really.'

'Perhaps if we all got what we deserved — ' She left the sentence uncompleted. She wiped the sweat from Walsh's face, then bent down and kissed him on the forehead.

He looked at her in surprise. 'Why did you do that?'

'I don't know,' she said. 'Are you angry?'

He shook his head. He seemed puzzled. 'No, not angry, Evelyn.' He stopped speaking, but his lips moved as though he were groping for words.

'Yes?'

He gripped her hand. 'You're very good to me,' he said again. 'When we get back — '

'Yes?'

'When we get back I'll see about that job. I won't forget.'

'Thank you,' she said.

He was looking at her as though he had only now really seen, her as though he were seeing her for the first time as a woman and not simply a stewardess.

* * *

Barlow heard the voices in the night, the chattering, gibbering voices of the jungle. And mingling with these he heard the voices of the ghosts. There were the ghosts of the dead village, of Lanyon; the ghosts of King and Copley, of Meade and Grimes and Helen Tudor; and behind them all the howling, grimacing phantom of madness.

Barlow fled before the ghosts; he fled into the darkness as Lanyon had fled, running with head down through the trailing vines, the dripping fronds and all the thick and sappy vegetation that tore at him with unseen, groping fingers.

He tripped and fell. He began to crawl

forward on his hands and knees. Drops of water showered down upon him; he could feel slime under his hands, slime on his face.

He crawled forward desperately and thought he heard the sound of pursuit. It goaded him forward even more frantically than before; he felt the urgent need to get away, to escape from the ghosts that were pushing him through this black world of nightmare.

And then suddenly it was lighter; he could see a ribbon of sky overhead and the glittering stars. He could see the stars scattered on the ground in front of him also; they moved, they changed into long spears of brilliance and shrank to tiny points of silvery gold. He heard the soft gurgle of water and his brain cleared from its fever as if the light in the jungle had brought light into his own mind.

'The river,' he muttered. 'It is the river. It is here. It was not a dream. It is here.'

He dipped his fingers into the water and splashed his face; he could have cried out in joy that he had found this guide for which he had so long been searching. And it had been the ghosts that had driven him to it; they had driven him through the night towards the river and had shown him where his pointer lay. Perhaps now they would leave him in peace.

He bent down and scooped up more water, and felt a hand touch his shoulder. He jerked round with an involuntary cry of returning terror; but it was only the girl. He could see the dim outline of her face in the starlight.

'You, Katie? What are you doing here?'

'I followed you,' she said. 'I saw you get up and run away. I was afraid. I thought — '

'What did you think?'

'It doesn't matter now.'

He stood up and put his hands on her arms. 'You thought I had gone mad, didn't you? Maybe I had. But it's finished now. Look, Katie; here is the river.'

'Yes,' she said. 'The river.'

'You see it's real. It wasn't something that I imagined.'

'I never thought it was. I believe in you.'

'Because you love me?'

'Perhaps because of that.'

He let his hands move round her body, drawing her to him. 'I love you too, Katie. I love you too.'

★ ★ ★

They were moving very slowly now, hampered by Walsh's bad leg. It took them five more days to reach the village. It was just as it had been when Barlow had seen it last. Nothing had changed.

They came out of the jungle like the last stragglers of a defeated army. Walsh was leaning on Miss Partridge's arm and Barlow was leading the way. They saw the huts, the decaying roofs, the encroaching growth, and the strange silence of the place struck them as a rush of dank air strikes the trespasser in a vault. All around were the noises of the jungle, but here in the village was only the silence of death.

'Let's move on,' Walsh said. 'Let's get away.'

'Don't you want to call on the inhabitants?' Barlow asked.

'There's nothing for us here. No help.'

'There could be.'

He wondered why he had not thought of it the first time when he had come with Lanyon; but then the impact of death and corruption had driven all else from his mind. Now it seemed so obvious: this village was close to the river and these had almost certainly been river people; therefore there would surely be canoes. It was simply a question of finding them.

'What do you mean?' Walsh asked. 'What help could there be?'

'Transport perhaps,'

* * *

The canoes had become grown over with vegetation, but they found them; heavy dug-outs made from the trunks of trees. There were paddles also.

'Transport,' Barlow said again. 'It was waiting for us all the time.'

'And where will it take us?' Walsh asked.

'It will take us where the river goes.'

'You will be able to rest your leg,' Miss Partridge said.

'Thank God for that.'

They left the choice of canoe to Barlow;

he was the seaman. It taxed their strength to heave it into the water, but it floated on an even keel and there was ample room in it.

They stepped into the canoe and pushed away from the bank. They paddled out into mid-stream and the current seized them and carried them away into the unknown.

21

The River

The river was a broad, thick, sinuous tongue on whose surface they slid almost without effort, using the paddles for scarcely any other purpose than that of steerage.

The jungle came close up to the river on either side, so that they were enclosed as by tall green walls, impenetrable to the eye. At the edges vines and creepers trailed in the water, branches thrust out their canopies of leaves, and slimy, weed-covered roots arched out of the mud like the rotting ribs of ancient ships.

The water was now brown, now grey, now black, its colour varying from moment to moment. It had an oily, glutted look, as though it had swallowed more than it could digest and were about to cast up the unwanted surplus. It was impossible to see below the surface, impossible to judge the depth, to guess what lay beneath the gliding bottom of the canoe. They moved in a kind of dream in the hot and humid atmosphere, unable to say what might lie beyond the next bend, unable to calculate by any means what distance they had travelled, to estimate how far they still must go. It was a journey to which there seemed to be no beginning and no end, as though they had been marooned on an island of time, an unchanging atom of space surrounded by the sliding water and the green enclosure of the forest walls.

The river murmured softly in a language they could not understand; eddies moved past them, concentric circles that tried to twist the canoe into their own orbits; here and there a saturated log floated half-submerged; here and there the log was alive, had eyes and jaws. Raucous, gaily-coloured birds stammered in the trees or swung out and away in a riot of flashing wings. The sun cast its shadows or stood above them in unchallenged majesty, burning the last remnants of energy from their starved and weary bodies. They lay in the canoe and drifted onward, dazed by the heat, bludgeoned by the sun, weakened by hunger.

'We are being watched,' Walsh muttered.

'Who could be watching us?' Miss Partridge asked.

'There are eyes — eyes everywhere — watching — watching.'

'There is only the jungle.'

She dipped a cloth in the water and bathed his forehead. He was becoming feverish; his mind was wandering. Perhaps it was the wound affecting him.

'Let me look at your leg,' she said.

He allowed her to roll the tattered pyjamas above his knee. The leg had swollen to almost twice its normal size; it looked dropsical. Miss Partridge untied the bandage that had been torn from Walsh's dressing-gown, and he gave a sharp cry of pain. The wound was suppurating and the bandage had become stuck to the leg. It gave off an unpleasant odour.

Miss Partridge washed the pus away with river water and replaced the bandage.

There was nothing else that could be done.

Barlow's arm was not healing either, but it was not nearly as bad as Walsh's leg. It was stiff certainly, but he could use it. He sat in the stern of the canoe and steered with a paddle, and the current took them on.

'The eyes,' Walsh muttered again. 'All those eyes — watching.'

'Now, now,' Miss Partridge said. 'You mustn't think about such things as that. It's just imagination, you know. There's nothing there.'

Barlow repeated softly: 'Nothing there? Can you be so certain of that?'

Miss Partridge looked at him reprovingly. 'Now, Mr Barlow, don't you start too. One is enough to deal with.'

'Good for you, Evelyn,' Barlow said. 'You're the one to keep us on the rails. No nonsense, eh? Everything perfectly normal with a perfectly normal explanation. No witchcraft, no mumbo-jumbo, no eyes watching. Nothing.'

'Precisely so. Just a river and some trees.'

'And the sun. Don't forget the sun. It never forgets us.'

The sun was hot and brassy, a blazing fire in the sky, a great shaft of heat thrusting through space with the one purpose of shrivelling them where they lay, floating upon the murky surface of the river. The air was still, as though it too had lost all energy to move. Only the water was alive, always shifting, rippling, eddying, swirling; only the water and perhaps something hidden behind the walls of the trees. Who could tell?

★ ★ ★

The hours passed and they did not count the hours. Days passed and they did not count the days.

'How much farther do you think we must go?' Katherine asked. 'Surely we must come to some kind of civilization soon.'

'There's no certainty about anything,' Barlow said. 'We lost all certainty when the *Southern Pioneer* went down. Since then we've been drifting, groping in

297

darkness. We may find something, maybe not. It's all a gamble.'

'We shall find something.'

'Of course we shall,' Miss Partridge said. 'We mustn't give in. We must keep up our spirits.'

'Didn't you forget something?' Barlow asked.

'What would that be?'

'Never say die.'

'It's the river of death,' Walsh muttered. 'How far do you have to travel on the river of death?' Suddenly he sat up; his eyes were brilliant and staring. He put out his hand and gripped Miss Partridge's arm with fierce strength. 'Have you got the money? Tell me, have you remembered to bring the money?'

'What money, Mr Walsh?'

'The coins for Charon. Charon must have his due.'

Miss Partridge patted his hand. 'There now; don't trouble your head about that. It's all taken care of. No need for you to worry.'

He sank back and his eyes lost their mad look. 'Good, good. I knew I could rely on you. You're a good secretary. The best I've ever had. It would not do to forget Charon.'

'He'll get no money from me,' Barlow said. 'Not a brass farthing.'

★ ★ ★

At nightfall they would move in to the bank and wait for morning, lying in the canoe, perhaps sleeping, perhaps not. Morning came with a mist over the river, a thin veil which the sun rent aside. This was the best time, the time of coolness and magic, of shrouded outlines and muted colours, a time that was neither night nor day, when the sounds were the small muffled sounds of water whispering past trailing leaves, of drops gently falling, of this whole river world taking a long breath before finally shaking off the clinging webs of sleep.

Too soon the sun reasserted its authority and the sky began to burn; the mist vanished and the canoe slid on through a haze of heat with its drowsy human cargo listlessly gazing at the unchanging panorama of river and trees and creepers.

There were hazards that threatened them — mud-banks, logs, underwater obstacles. Sometimes the canoe would become stuck fast and it would be long before it was free again; sometimes it almost capsized; but always they passed the danger and went on.

They had to watch Walsh; there was a fever burning in him now. For long periods he shook with ague and his eyes were unnaturally bright. Occasionally he would start up in delirium and it was all they could do to restrain him; then he would relapse into a kind of coma and lie like a dead man in the bottom of the canoe.

'Mr Walsh is getting near the end of his tether,' Barlow said. He was thinking that they were all near the end.

'He is not going to die,' Miss Partridge said. She had struggled for Walsh so long and so devotedly that she refused to let him go now. She felt for him more than mere love; indeed she herself scarcely realized the intensity of her feeling for this wasted, pain-racked wreck of a man. She felt a burning desire to snatch him back from death, to build in him again the strength and character that he had once possessed, to make of him again a true and proper man.

'He must not die,' she said. 'I will not allow him to die.'

'None of us can control life and death,' Barlow said.

He had started to dream now; even by day he dreamed. He dreamed that they were all in the canoe as they had been in the boat, all thirteen of them.

'Thirteen is an unlucky number,' he said.

Katherine gazed at him, loving him and fearing for him. For herself she had no more fear, but for him she feared always.

'There are only four of us now,' she said. 'We began with thirteen but now there are only four.'

'Thirteen is an unlucky number. It's unlucky like walking under ladders or whistling in a ship. You have to know these things.'

'Superstition,' Miss Partridge said firmly. 'Nothing but primitive superstition.'

'This is a primitive country.'

★   ★   ★

None of them could remember when they first heard the drums. It was an insidious sound that seemed to creep up on them unawares. And perhaps in truth there were no drums; perhaps it was a sound only in their own heads, a pulse beating.

They did not speak to one another of the drums, allowing that soft throbbing to pass over them like the humming of bees, unremarked.

But each one believed now that they were being watched, that beyond the wall of jungle fringeing the banks of the river were flitting shadows that kept pace with them, gliding through the green shade as unhindered by solid obstacles as a moving spectre or a puff of smoke. It was no longer Walsh only who imagined these things, but all of them. But they did not speak of them. They kept the secret of the watching eyes, as they kept the secret of the drums, hidden in the deep recesses of their own minds.

★ ★ ★

Barlow lay in the canoe and dreamed. Ahead of him was Katherine, ahead of her, Miss Partridge. Walsh lay with his eyes closed, his leg swollen and discoloured like a monstrous German sausage.

The canoe drifted without guidance, without purpose, turning this way and that as the current took it. The river had widened and the banner of the sky was wider also, a great blue slit in the roof of trees. Sometimes Barlow looked at the sky, sometimes he closed his eyes. He felt an overpowering lassitude that was almost a sensuous pleasure. The smallest effort, the mere raising of an arm, was something that had to be considered for a long time, considered and then abandoned. The drums were a gentle throbbing in the distance.

Barlow dreamed that the canoe was no longer alone. On either side of it were other canoes filled with dark, shining bodies, heads with piled crinkly hair like great wigs, broad nose with bones pushed through them, necklaces of cowrie shells, tattoo marks, gleaming muscles, gleaming teeth.

He did not move. He let the dream carry him on, unresisting. He dreamed that there was a kind of jetty, that the canoe was pushed in towards this jetty, that beyond the jetty were houses, some thatched, some with roofs of corrugated iron. He dreamed that a man in khaki shorts and a bush shirt was looking down at him.

The man said: 'My name's Watkins. You seem to have had a bad time. Where have you come from?'

'From a ship,' Barlow said.

'A ship? Yes, well we'll talk about that later.'

And then he was being lifted out of the canoe and carried along the jetty towards a house with a white-painted roof and a broad verandah. He was making no effort, not even trying to understand, because in a dream there was no need for

304

understanding, no need for logic.

Behind him he heard the man Watkins talking: 'They're pretty far gone. Don't look as if they've eaten for weeks. Come from a ship? Delirious.'

He wanted to tell Watkins that he was not delirious, but it was not worth the effort. He allowed himself to be carried into the house.

22

Gone Away

The Reverend Joseph Watkins steered the motor dinghy in towards the beach with all the skill of a professional sailor. As he sat at the tiller his exceptional height was masked, but when he was standing he topped Barlow by a good six inches. He had a thin, lined face and greying hair. He looked what he was — a dedicated man; dedicated to the task of spreading the word of Christ among a primitive people.

'Three of them, you said, Chris?'

'That's all. And they're not armed. They'll be no trouble.'

'I was not expecting trouble,' Mr Watkins said with a smile. He had a sharp-edged lower jaw, slightly jutting, and a neck like a bundle of old rope.

Astern of them the yacht in which they had come lay at anchor, utterly motionless.

'You will go back to the sea, I suppose?' Watkins said.

Barlow shook his head. 'I'm leaving it — for good.'

'Why is that?'

'The sea is all right for a man who's single. When he's married it's not so good.'

'And you are thinking of getting married?'

'Yes.'

The sea was perfectly calm. The racket of the dinghy's engine was a solitary sound in an expanse of silence. The two men were the only occupants of the boat and behind them a white trail of foam widened like the head of an arrow.

'To Miss Summers?' Watkins asked.

'Yes.'

'I congratulate you. She seems an admirable young lady.'

'Walsh has offered me a job. I may take it.'

Watkins tilted his head on one side and his eyes narrowed.

'What kind of relationship is there

307

between Mr Walsh and Miss Partridge, would you say?'

'Devotion on one side, acceptance of that devotion on the other. I think she would make him a very good nurse.'

'Not a wife?'

'Maybe that too. You think his leg will heal?'

'Oh, yes. Already it is much less swollen. I don't think we need worry about him any more. He's beginning to be bad-tempered and that's always a good sign. Wants to get in touch with a man called Jackson. Some enemy of his, judging by the language.'

'It's his partner,' Barlow said.

They went up the beach together and no one came to meet them. They found the remains of the semi-circle of skulls and the rough seat of judgement that King had had erected. They saw the long-dead ashes of the fire and the empty rum barrel.

'There's something written here,' Watkins said.

Barlow looked at the barrel and saw two words roughly carved on it. The message was brief.

'Gone away.'

He looked up towards the mountain where he knew the three idols were standing, and he inclined his head slightly before turning away.

'You've got it to yourselves again,' he said.

THE END

Other titles in the
Linford Mystery Library

A LANCE FOR THE DEVIL
Robert Charles

The funeral service of Pope Paul VI was to be held in the great plaza before St. Peter's Cathedral in Rome, and was to be the scene of the most monstrous mass assassination of political leaders the world had ever known. Only Counter-Terror could prevent it.

TOO LATE FOR THE FUNERAL
Roger Ormerod

Carol Turner, seventeen, and a mystery, is very close to a murder, and she has in her possession a weapon that could prove a number of things. But it is Elsa Mallin who suffers most before the truth of Carol Turner releases her.

IN THAT RICH EARTH
Alan Sewart
How long does it take for a human body to decay until only the bones remain? When Detective Sergeant Harry Chamberlane received news of a body, he raised exactly that question. But whose was the body? Who was to blame for the death and in what circumstances?

THE MARGIN
Ian Stuart
It is rumoured that Walkers Brewery has been selling arms to the South African army, and Graham Lorimer is asked to investigate. He meets the beautiful Shelley van Rynveld, who is dedicated to ending apartheid. When a Walkers employee is killed in a hit-and-run accident, his wife tells Graham that he's been seeing Shelley van Rynveld . . .

NIGHT OF THE FAIR
Jay Baker

The gun was the last of the things for which Harry Judd had fought and now it was in the hands of his worst enemy, aimed at the boy he had tried to help. This was the night in which the past had to be faced again and finally understood.

BOMB SCARE — FLIGHT 147
Peter Chambers

Smog delayed Flight 147, and so prevented a bomb exploding in mid-air. Walter Keane found that during the crisis he had been robbed of his jewel bag, and Mark Preston was hired to locate it without involving the police. When a murder was committed, Preston knew the stake had grown.

SALVAGE JOB
Bill Knox
A storm has left the oil tanker S. S. *Craig Michael* stranded and almost blocking the only channel to the bay at Cabo Esco. Sent to investigate, marine insurance inspector Laird discovers that the Portuguese bay is hiding a powder keg of international proportions.

DEATH OF A MARINE
Charles Leader
When Mike M'Call found the mutilated corpse of a marine in an alleyway in Singapore, a thousand-strong marine battalion was hell-bent on revenge for their murdered comrade — and the next target for the tong gang of paid killers appeared to be M'Call himself . . .

THE SUN VIRGIN
Robert Charles

A search for Inca gold was the challenge held out to Peter Conway by his brother Steve. What Steve forgot to mention was that the man whom Peter was to replace on the expedition had already been murdered — and there was more than one interested party ready to lie, steal and even kill for the Inca fortune.

CART BEFORE THE HEARSE
Roger Ormerod

Sometimes a case comes up backwards. When Ernest Connelly said 'I have killed . . . ', he did not name the victim. So Dave Mallin and George Coe find themselves attempting to discover a body to fit the crime.